CONTENTS

KIRA

PREQUEL TO THE YDEN TRILOGY

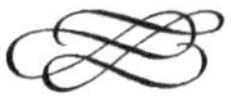

SUZANNE G. ROGERS

IDUNN COURT PUBLISHING

GLOSSARY & PRONUNCIATION GUIDE

Aion (eye-on)—young Nomad warrior

Cheernaught (*cheer*-not)—a town in the southwestern part of Nomad Territory

Cygard (*sigh*-gard)—a heavily armored Cyclops who works as a mercenary. Cygards served as Warlord Mandral's army

Dorsit (*door*-sit)—handsome and creative Leopard Clan wizard, close friend and ally to the Dragon Clan

Efysian (eff-*e*-see-in)—sinister Wolf Clan wizard

Gnoam (nome)—former warlord turned Governor

Hafne (**haff**-nee)—a vendor with a food stall in Mandral Village

Hyrn (hern)—young Nomad warrior

Isore (*i*-zore)—cygard soldier who becomes a captain in Mandral's army

Kira (*kir*-ah)—extremely beautiful daughter of President Szul, and Jon's friend

Kysandra (kiss-*an*-drah)—Kira's elder sister

Lianyn (lee-*an*-in)—nomad scout

Lunegra (loon-*eh*-grah)—largest of Yden's two moons

Lunendra (loon-*in*-drah)—smaller of Yden's two moons

Mandral (man-*drall*)—former ruthless warlord of Mandral Territory

Moala (mo-*all*-ah)—a merchant who deals in illegal artifacts

Newtic (*new*-tick)—small, furry rodent that pops when touched

Patnik (*pat*-nick)—Turtle Clan wizard

Porcinian (por-*sin*-ee-an)—wild hog, resembling a boar

Puleden (*pull*-eh-den)—beast of burden with a tail like an elephant's trunk

Quixoran (kicks-*or*-an)—powerful patriarch of the Dragon Clan

Rampen Szul (*ramp*-in zool)— Chief of the Nomads and Kira's father

Reye (ray)—handsome Nomad warrior in President Szul's elite Special Guards

Solegra (sol-*eh*-grah)—the larger of Yden's two suns

Solendra (sol-*en*-drah)—the smaller of Yden's two suns

Spyrrow (*spy*-row)—a magical spy bird that can transmit images to a spyball

Teryn (*terr*-in)—the name of Kira's mother

Tyrg (teerg)—thin, bald scribe

Wyckcrest (*wick*-crest)—a village outside of Castle Ytherium, formerly known as Mandral Village

Yden (*ee*-den)—a magical planet in an alternate dimension

Ylan (ee-lann—local pronunciation is *lann*)—charming seaside village on Ylan Bay, the body of water where Dragon Isle is located. Birthplace, Dorsit of the Leopard Clan

Yrth (earth)—third planet from the sun. Sometimes referred to on Yden as Hell, the planet without magic

THE INVASION

*A*s teams of puledens hauled carts westward through the mountain pass, the creaking of the wagon wheels echoed off of granite cliffs. Two men on horseback led the small convoy into the gathering twilight. As they crested yet another rise, Mandral reined in his horse and gave his companion a withering glance.

"Wizard, I'm beginning to think these Cyclopes don't exist."

Patnik chuckled. "Of course they do, Warlord. They've been following us for the last hour."

Mandral scanned his surroundings but saw only hundreds of boulders. "Why don't they show themselves?"

"They're in plain sight, if you know what to look for."

The wizard fashioned an everlasting orb of light between his hands. When he sent it aloft, a deep rumble began, like the sound of an earthquake. As Mandral peered out over the cold, windswept landscape, boulders began to move closer. The illumination from the everlasting orb revealed the enormous creatures at last—largely naked even in the freezing cold. Twice the size of men, with pus-filled lesions over their bodies, the

Cyclopes surrounded the wagons and fixed Mandral with their single eyes.

"Show no fear," Patnik murmured.

"Watch yourself, wizard," Mandral said. "I don't need your advice, just your magic."

He rode back toward the wagons, loosened their covering tarps, and flung them aside. In one wagon, jugs of ale were stacked in neat rows. In the second, piles of animal skins along with dried meat, bags of salt, and baskets of vegetables formed a tempting display. As the Cyclopes pressed forward, the warlord unsheathed his sword and swept it in a warning arc. The creatures hesitated.

"I bring gifts and an offer. Who speaks for the Cyclopes?"

A brutish hairy creature pushed his way to the front of the crowd.

"Keep your offer, human. We'll take the gifts."

A frenzy ensued as the Cyclopes nearly tore the carts apart in their zeal to grab what lay inside. Mandral was obliged to gallop to a safe distance clear of the fray. Patnik had a worried expression as he joined him.

"My apologies, Warlord. I'm afraid the Cyclopes aren't used to dealing with humans."

"All will be well." Mandral smirked as he sheathed his sword.

"Perhaps you should keep your weapon at the ready. Even a shield spell won't hold these brutes back forever." He gulped. "In fact, we should depart with all due haste. After the carts are empty, the Cyclopes may attack."

Unconcerned, the warlord made no reply. When the jugs of ale were uncorked and the Cyclopes drank freely, he gave a satisfied nod.

"The Cyclopes are mine."

The wizard gasped. "Is the ale poisoned?"

"Naturally. It's a rather devious concoction which brings about euphoria, followed closely by an overwhelming sense of devotion. Amongst women, it's mistaken for passionate adoration." He paused. "There is no cure."

Moments later, the Cyclopes rushed toward Mandral, with outstretched hands. Patnik flinched.

"Show no fear, wizard," Mandral drawled.

One by one, the Cyclopes sank to their knees, including the hairy Cyclops who'd spoken. Mandral's lips curved into a smile.

"My name is Warlord Mandral."

The name was slavishly repeated by the Cyclopes, like a mantra or a prayer. Patnik chuckled and slid the warlord a silent look of admiration.

"I've come to invade Nomad Territory." Mandral paused for effect. "And you're my army."

SPARRING

Gant finally brought Kira down with a scissor tackle. As her upper back slammed into the hard dirt surface of the forest floor, an invisible iron hand seemed to grab her lungs and squeeze. Unable to breathe, she curled up into a fetal position and gasped for air. Gant lay beside her on the ground, his eyes closed.

"Stay down, Kira," Gant muttered. "I'm done."

His attempt to rise was futile. A moan escaped his lips, and he collapsed into a heap. Moments later, the trees overhead began to rain Nomads. The young warriors knelt next to Gant and felt for his pulse.

"Is he all right?" Kira managed.

"Just passed out," Aion said. "He'll be all right in a few minutes."

Kira's lungs finally eased their spasms, and she managed to draw a deep breath. "Doesn't anyone care about me?"

"No," Hyrn said.

General laughter followed his remark.

"You train too hard, Kira Szul," Aion said. "The Nomads

aren't under attack and there's no threat of war, so why do you take it so seriously?"

She raised herself up on her elbows. "Training isn't supposed to be a game!"

"Nothing's a game to you," Lane said. "You wouldn't know how to have fun even if you tried."

"Not every contest needs to be to the death," Hyrn said. "Gant may have won the match just now, but he nearly killed himself doing it."

As if he'd heard his name, Gant began to stir. The three Nomads hauled him upright and practically carried him through the forest on their way back to the encampment. Lane and Aion shot level glances at Kira as they went, which didn't escape her notice. She made her way to a downed log and sat, waiting for her lungs to fully resume their normal function.

By any estimation, her friends' lack of concern for her wasn't fair. Before Gant had fainted, he'd left a bruise the size of Nomad Territory on her thigh. He'd also nearly dislocated her shoulder, and her ribs were sore from where he'd landed a brutal side kick. All those injuries were in addition to a myriad of scrapes she'd sustained from sticks, stones, and pinecones as they grappled across the forest floor. Admittedly, her injuries mightn't have been so severe if she hadn't pushed him so hard, but as Rampen Szul's daughter she couldn't afford to slack off.

When Kira wiped sweat from her face, her fingertips came away bloody from a cut on her scalp. She groaned as she remembered—too late—her elder sister's birthday celebration that night. Nothing she ever did could please Kysandra on a normal day. If she couldn't get cleaned up before her sister noticed, a fresh volley of criticism would ensue. Since they shared a tent together, the chances of escaping her sister's pointed scrutiny were slim.

On her way back to the Nomad encampment, Kira spied several young men in a clearing, laughing and talking as they tossed knives at a target. Her stomach contracted when she noticed a shock of blond hair; the young warrior Reye was among the group. His handsome face and athletic frame had earned him a reputation among Nomad women as a desirable marriage partner...yet he continued to elude capture. At only fifteen turns of age, Kira was still too young to contemplate marriage, but privately she'd admired Reye along with the rest. She'd had few opportunities to talk with him, but now was her opening. Her fingers itched to best the lads at target practice and socialize with Reye at the same time. As soon as she stepped toward the clearing, however, a fragment of conversation made her pause.

"So, Reye, which girl are you escorting to Kysandra's party?"

"Must I choose only one?"

Raucous laughter greeted Reye's flippant response.

"I heard Kira Szul is in need of an escort."

The words sounded innocent enough, but Kira detected an undercurrent of mockery.

"Ha! You take her." Reye lifted his hands, as if in fright. "I'm too afraid."

"Oh, come now. She's little more than a child."

"She always looks like she wants to kick someone's teeth in. Besides which, I prefer my women soft, with curves." He pantomimed an hourglass figure with his hands.

"If it's voluptuous you want, choose a nymph."

"Again, must I choose only one?"

More laughter ensued. Stung, Kira faded back into the shadows. Her throat closed up as she felt the full impact of Reye's scorn, and moisture filled her eyes. Until now, she hadn't realized she'd become a topic for ridicule. Her vision blurred with tears as she stumbled along the path toward her tent. Before she went in, however, she tried to compose herself. If Kysandra knew she was feeling vulnerable, no doubt she'd go for the jugular.

Olive green, fuzzy mountain-spider silk fashioned the walls and peaked roof of the tented dwelling, which provided ample shelter from the wind, rain, and occasional frost. Kira passed through the opening, hoping Kysandra was elsewhere. Her sister sat at her dressing table, unfortunately, arranging her hair.

Kysandra caught sight of Kira in the looking glass. "You're filthy!"

She examined her reflection. Her puleden-leather breaches and dragon-hide tunic were smeared with mud and grass stains, and leaves were sticking out from her tightly braided hair. Only her full lips and the unusual violet color of her eyes gave any hint of the girl hidden underneath the dirt.

Nevertheless, she shrugged. "I was sparring."

"You *always* look like that!"

"No, I don't."

"Maybe you're not always as dirty, but you always look like a boy. If it's not sparring, it's fighting with swords or throwing knives or axes or insults."

"We're Nomads. That's what we do."

"Nonsense. You're the Nomad Chief's youngest daughter, not his son."

"I know, but I have to train harder to get respect!"

"It's not working, and it's obvious to everyone you're trying too hard. You should hear how people talk about you behind your back."

There was truth in what Kysandra said, and it hurt Kira turned her back to hide the moisture rimming her eyes. With a sound of disgust, her sister stormed over to a wardrobe, pulled out a lace-edged garment, and tossed it onto Kira's bed.

"What's that for?"

"It's to replace that stupid combat binder you're wearing. From now on, you're to look like a girl. Take a change of clothes down to the hot spring and scrub before anyone sees or smells you. And let your hair down for Solegra's sake!"

Ordinarily Kira would be inured to her sister's harsh assessments, but Reye's comments had already opened a wound. Feeling ill-used, she gathered her things together.

"Oh, and Father has invited some guests to my party. You're to wear a dress."

"Who are the guests?"

"Warlord Laramy and some of his soldiers. Although I've never met the man, I'm told Laramy is not altogether ill-favored. I intend to marry him, if possible."

AT THE HOT SPRING, Kira stripped off her clothes, loosened her tight braids, and dove into the pool. Since men were required to bath in the river on the far side of the encampment, she was assured of privacy. The crystal clear water was warm enough to release curls of steam into the air, and Kira felt her muscles relax and her aches lessen. She rubbed liquid soap into her scalp and skin, letting the clear water carry the bubbles away. The fragrant lilac soap was her own concoction. Infused with various essential oils, it left her skin and hair clean and allowed her to comb her hair afterward without snarls.

Once she'd scrubbed away the dirt and blood, she floated on her back with her eyes closed and tried unsuccessfully to forestall a crushing sense of loneliness. Although she'd devoted herself to training as a warrior her entire life, she'd begun to chafe at the role. Lately, she'd begun to notice men and to wish they'd notice her. *But I'm a warrior, and the only thing I know how to do is to fight.*

Never before had Kira felt the lack of maternal guidance so keenly. Kirana Teryn Szul had died giving birth to her, so Kira had no memories of her mother whatsoever. She pictured the small painting of her mother next to her bed. As a child, she used to talk to the image when nobody was around and wish her mother would respond. Eager for advice about men, Kira would have even welcomed the counsel of a water nymph at the moment. The few nymphs who'd lived in the hot spring had decamped for the river, however, when they realized where the males could be found. Usually she avoided the flirtatious nymphs, but they *did* have a knack for displaying their charms. Although she wasn't about to prance around stark naked, she could stand to make a few changes. For one thing, she could wear her long dark hair loose and unbraided. Furthermore, Kysandra was right; she didn't have to wear her combat binder all the time. Her sister had given her a binder designed to enhance her blossoming femininity instead of hiding it. Reye was a lost cause, evidently, but he wasn't the only handsome Nomad warrior in the Territory. Perhaps she could also learn to conduct a pleasant conversation about something other than swordplay or combat.

An unfamiliar masculine voice shattered her reverie.

"Are you a water nymph?"

Startled, Kira jackknifed under the water and came up for air as far away from the voice as possible. Unfortunately, the pool was surrounded by ten soldiers on horseback, each equipped with swords, chain mail, and leers.

"You're the prettiest nymph we've seen yet."

"Come on out and talk to us, little one."

Just then a warrior appeared astride an enormous charger. "What's happening here?"

"We're talking to a water nymph, Warlord."

Warlord Laramy!

"She's no nymph. The girl's a Nomad, and we're intruding on her privacy." Laramy smiled at Kira and bowed his head. "Please forgive our bad manners, but we're looking for the Nomad encampment at Wyckcrest."

"If you take the path through the woods, you'll reach the encampment in ten minutes."

"Thank you."

As Laramy spurred his charger forward, he gave Kira a lingering glance. When the soldiers finally disappeared beyond the tree line, she let out the breath she'd been holding. Nevertheless, she didn't fully emerge from the water until her fingertips and toes had shriveled.

She left off her combat binder and donned the new one, reveling in a newfound freedom of movement. After dressing in a fresh pair of breeches and a blouse, she combed her hair, letting the sunshine dry her wavy, waist-length mane. As she worked, she couldn't stop scanning the forest for the reappearance of Laramy's men. She'd let down her guard by coming to the hot spring without a weapon. *From now on I won't bathe without a stiletto strapped to my thigh.*

LANE WAS PACING out front of Kira's tent when she returned. He gaped openly at her unleashed hair and figure.

"What's wrong?" she asked.

"I almost didn't recognize you with your hair down and everything. Um…your father has sent for you. He'd like you to greet a visitor."

"Warlord Laramy?"

"How'd you know?"

"I met him and his party as they rode in." Kira paused. "Look, please tell Gant I'm sorry about our sparring this morning. I took it too far and I regret it."

Lane nodded. "I'll tell him. You know, you really need to learn to relax."

"Yeah. See you later."

Kira stashed her belongings and walked toward her father's tent without delay. Inside, Rampen Szul was enjoying a mug of ale with Warlord Laramy and Kysandra. Her father did a double take when she appeared.

"Ah, come meet our guest, Warlord Laramy. He and his men will be staying with us for a fortnight. Warlord, this is my youngest daughter, Kira."

Laramy stood, and his smirk told her he recognized her from their encounter at the hot spring. For her part, Kira pretended not to notice.

"Welcome to Nomad Territory."

"Thank you. I consider myself fortunate to be here." Laramy glanced at Szul. "You're favored to have two such beautiful daughters."

At that, Kysandra's eyes narrowed and her lips became thin. Taken aback at her sister's obvious ire, Kira was mystified as to what she'd done wrong. Kysandra gave Laramy a gracious, forced smile as she rose.

"I'm afraid Kira and I must leave you gentlemen to your ale. We must ready ourselves for my birthday celebration."

Outside, Kysandra would say nothing until they were safely inside their own tent. Then she unleashed her fury. "Have you no shame, flaunting yourself in front of the warlord like a common nymph?"

"What?"

"Your blouse is too revealing!"

When Kira glanced down at her attire, her face warming with embarrassment. She'd failed to make allowances for the effects of the new binder on her burgeoning figure, and she did in fact resemble a nymph.

"I'm sorry. I was summoned immediately on my return from the hot spring and I didn't have the chance to dress appropriately. It wasn't on purpose."

"Wasn't it?" Kysandra's tone was clipped. "Stay away from Warlord Laramy. I intend to pursue him, even if it means buying a love potion from Marybell in the village."

"Love potions are illegal, and Marybell would never deal in something so despicable!"

"I'm only joking."

"What about your engagement to Dorsit?"

"He's not coming back, and at one and twenty turns I'm not getting any younger. For all we know, Dorsit is dead."

Kira averted her eyes. "Don't say that."

"He wasn't the sort of wizard to run off without a word to his intended bride. Undoubtedly the wizard Efysian killed him."

A shudder went through Kira at the thought of the evil Wolf Clan wizard. Few had ever seen the man, but the effects of his decades-long rampage had been felt by all. Friendly dragons associated with the Dragon Clan used to flock across the skies, but they'd fallen victim to Efysian's fury. Wizards from all clans had vanished, one by one, and now only the old and relatively weak remained. Although Dorsit of the Leopard Clan was young and powerful, he'd supposed himself safe in Nomad Territory. Yet he had also disappeared, and Efysian, who should have been an unpleasant memory turns ago, continued to terrorize Yden.

"I wish we knew what happened to Dorsit," Kira said.

Kysandra lowered her voice. "They say many wizards fled Efysian by transporting to the planet without magic."

"That's just a myth to frighten children. There is no such place as Yrth." She paused. "I miss Dorsit terribly."

"I don't." Unexpectedly, her sister laughed. "I'm not sure I could have been happy with a man prettier than me. Anyway, he couldn't have been much of a wizard if he let Efysian get the better of him."

Kira's temper rose. "That's the stupidest thing I've ever heard. I loved Dorsit like a brother, and I won't listen to your insults."

She grabbed the curtain gathered at one side of the tent and drew it closed.

QUEST

As she readied herself for the party, Kira tried to regain her good humor. Since she had no interest in attracting Laramy's admiration, her sister's jealousy was baseless. The warlord was handsome enough, and possessed fine manners, but he was far too old for her. Truth be told, she was keen for Kysandra to wed the warlord. If that fortunate event were to occur, her sister would journey north to Laramy Territory, likely never to return. She couldn't encourage Kysandra enough...although her enthusiasm stopped short of endorsing the use of a so-called love potion.

Because her sister would be wearing an eye-catching red velvet gown shot with gold embroidery, Kira chose a simple white dress handed down from her mother instead. The sash was faded and frayed, so she replaced it with a girdle woven from silver thread. She brushed her hair until it shone and left it loose and unadorned. The only cosmetic Kira used was a moisturizing pomade on her lips, although she did comb a little of the pomade into her thick eyebrows to ensure they were tamed and sleek. Her eyes slid to the painting of Kirana Teryn Szul. Her mother had been a famous beauty, by all accounts.

Was Kira worthy to be called her daughter? With a sigh, she picked up her sister's birthday gift and left the tent to join the party.

A large open-air pavilion had been erected in the center of the encampment for the birthday celebration. As lively music played, people hastened to join the throngs of dancers already assembled. To one side, long wooden tables were laden with all manner of dishes, from roast puleden to sugared fruits. Kysandra's birthday gifts filled another table, and Kira nestled her offering—a bottle of rose fragrance she'd mixed herself—amongst the others. Many people stared as she filled a wooden trencher with a variety of food. She imagined it was because nobody had ever seen her dress like a girl before. Self-conscious, she slid into a seat at her father's table and tried to ignore the unwanted attention.

While she ate, she enjoyed an unobstructed view of the dance floor, where her sister was dancing with the guest of honor. Nearby, her father partnered elderly Nanna Cranburry. After the dance ended, Szul escorted Nanna from the dance floor while Laramy ushered Kysandra back to her seat. The color of Kysandra's dress flattered her face, in Kira's opinion, and her elaborate hair arrangement drew attention to her blue eyes. Kira was suddenly quite glad she'd dressed in a simple fashion; her sister would have no cause for jealousy or complaint. When Laramy passed Kira, however, his gaze lingered overly long. Although she glanced away, he was seemingly not dissuaded. Moments later, he strode over to her and sketched a courtly bow.

"Would you do me the honor of dancing with me, Princess?"

Unable to refuse a guest of her father's, Kira accompanied the warlord to the dance floor for a reel. Thereafter, she did not sit down again until the musicians took a short break. Laramy danced with her several times, and then his men jockeyed amongst themselves to be her next partner. *They, at least, are not afraid of me!* When Kira finally slid into her seat, breathless and laughing, Kysandra cut her merriment short.

"You'll retire now. I'll give your apologies to our guests."

She was stung. "Why must I retire?"

"Father and I've both agreed you've developed a headache."

Kira's gaze slid to her father several yards away. When their eyes met, he gave her a firm nod. Inwardly, she was incensed, but she had little choice. Without another word, she returned to her tent. *It's not fair, and I didn't even have any cake!* She threw herself across her bed, wondering what on Yden she'd done to be sent away like a naughty child. Her mulish expression remained when her father joined her several minutes later.

"I didn't do anything wrong!" she exclaimed. "And if Kysandra said I did, she's not being truthful!"

To her surprise, her father's smile was sympathetic. "Of course you did nothing wrong, child, other than grow up overnight. Unfortunately, your beauty is diverting attention from your elder sister."

"My *beauty!*" Kira gasped. "I don't mean any disrespect, but you may have had too much wine."

He chuckled. "Not at all. I confess, when you appeared in that dress tonight, you took my breath away. You've no idea how much you look like your mother, who was one of the most beautiful women on Yden." He turned his head until he gazed at her mother's image. "I met Kirana Teryn when she was about your age, you know, and was completely smitten. We had to wait until she turned sixteen to wed."

Stunned, Kira could think of nothing to say. Is my father playing a cruel joke, or has regard for me dimmed his vision?

"Kysandra is pretty, but she can't hope to compete for Laramy with you nearby," Szul continued. "Therefore, I'm sending you for an extended visit with your cousins in Cheernaught. You'll leave tomorrow morning with Reye as your escort."

She made no attempt to hide her disdain. "Reye is a pule-den's behind and I'd rather die than spend five minutes in his company."

"He's my best warrior, Kira."

"*I'm* your best warrior, Father. I can handle myself."

"I'm not sending my extraordinarily beautiful young daughter out into the wilderness without an escort, and that's final." He tossed a small leather money pouch onto her bed. Judging by the way it fell, the pouch was heavier than it looked. "That gold will more than cover your expenses during the journey."

"But—"

"You'll leave after breakfast, Kira, and that's my final word."

KYSANDRA ENTERED THE TENT GIGGLING, but her happy demeanor quickly changed in Kira's presence. Although Kira wanted desperately to get a few hours' sleep, she was forced to listen to her sister's lengthy diatribe about her supposedly inappropriate choice of dress and flirtatious manner.

"Oh, hold your tongue! I was polite, not flirtatious, and there was nothing wrong with the gown," Kira shot back. "Why must you always be so critical?"

"Nobody gave you permission to wear my mother's clothes."

Kira recoiled. "I didn't think anyone had to give me permission! After all, she was my mother too."

"She died giving birth to you, so you didn't know her." Kysandra's tone was accusatory.

"You act like her death was my fault."

"Well, it *was*, wasn't it? Not a day goes by I don't miss her. I'd trade you for her without a moment's hesitation if I could, and I'm not the only one. I've heard Father say so too, when he's in his cups."

Kira knew that last part was a lie, but it hurt anyway. Her father had always been closer to her than to her sister, a fact which had probably rankled Kysandra along with every other complaint. The depth of her sister's hatred took Kira's breath away, and any lingering affection she'd ever harbored disappeared completely—as if it had never existed.

"You're such a horrible shrew, I feel sorry for Warlord Laramy."

Angrily, Kira drew the privacy curtain. As she lay in bed, she blotted bitter, hot tears away with the sleeve of her nightdress.

I can't wait to leave.

SOLEGRA HAD JUST PEEKED over the horizon when Kira crept from her tent with a knapsack in hand. She'd left a note of farewell on her bed addressed to her father, telling him she was bound for Cheernaught. That was true, in a roundabout way. Nothing in her message indicated she intended to stop in Ylan first, which was in the opposite direction. She was determined to visit Dorsit's hometown first, to see if she could discover what had become of him. *Perhaps Kysandra can forget her former intended easily, but I can't be so disloyal!* The detour would double her travel time, but who was to know or care? Cousins Abatha and Leeland wouldn't be expecting her until she arrived, and nobody at the Wyckcrest encampment would be overly concerned if she ever returned—except her father.

It would be several hours yet before anyone else stirred from their beds, but Kira nevertheless crept as quietly as possible to the steward's storehouse tent to fill a saddlebag with fruit, bread, and cheese. In the stables, she saddled a dapple gray mare called Myst, and led her by the bridle through the encampment in an easterly direction. When she was out of earshot, she swung herself up into the saddle and spurred Myst into a trot.

Safely nestled inside its scabbard, her newly sharpened sword jounced against her thigh in a comforting rhythm. She wore black breeches fashioned from a form-fitting fabric, a soft leather tunic, and a jacket equipped with a dozen small throwing knives sewn into the lining. In addition, two stilettos were secreted in her boots. *Hardly a helpless female!*

Kira directed Myst onto the main thoroughfare connecting the east and west borders of Nomad Territory. Although the road was deserted at present, local farmers and merchants would soon arrive as they delivered goods to Wyckcrest Village marketplace. The early morning air seemed to energize Myst, but Kira kept her to a fast walk. With such a long way to go, she didn't want the horse to tire too quickly. A week's ride lay ahead of her as she journeyed toward the eastern mountain range. Then, after she reached the river, her route would turn south for another three or four days.

Her growling stomach reminded Kira she'd not yet eaten. Just as she reached toward her saddlebag, two unsavory men leaped into the road with swords drawn. She reined Myst in. "Step aside."

"Hand over your money bag, lass, and we won't hurt ye."

Kira sighed inwardly, even as her hand moved inside her jacket. "I've no wish to kill you before breakfast. Toss your swords to the ground and back away."

The men exchanged a glance and laughed. After a moment, Kira joined in—which bewildered the robbers at first, but then made them angry. No sooner had they stepped toward her when she hurled a pair of throwing knives. The men crumpled to the dirt, clutching their throats. Too late, she saw a third highwayman armed with a bow and arrow, perched in a tree. As he pulled back his bowstring, a flash of silver hurtled past Kira's shoulder and embedded itself in the man's chest. With a gurgling cry, the archer fell from the tree and landed on a briar bush.

Kira drew her sword and glanced around. To her shock, Reye rode from the forest.

"How did you find me!" she exclaimed.

"Well, that's a fine thank you. I'd hoped to stay hidden a little longer, but it looked like you needed me."

He dismounted to retrieve her throwing knives. After wiping them on the robbers' clothes, he returned the razor-sharp weapons to her. "Good aim."

"Yours as well." She paused. "Thank you for your assistance."

"Think nothing of it."

Reye reclaimed his own knife, dragged the two corpses off the road, and gave Kira a measured glance. "I've been tracking you since you left the encampment. You're riding in the wrong direction."

Sunlight glinted on Kira's sword as she pointed it at him. "I'm not going back, so don't try to stop me."

He held up his hands in surrender. "Relax. Mortal combat would not end well for either of us."

She sheathed her sword. "If you don't intend to take me back, why are you here?"

"I was assigned to be your escort, not your jailer."

"What an unfortunate assignment for you."

Kira spurred Myst on, sending Reye scrambling for his horse. After he'd caught up, he matched her pace. After a few minutes, he glanced over. "Did you enjoy yourself at the party last night?"

"You were assigned to be my escort, not my confidant."

"There's nothing wrong with a little pleasant conversation to pass the time."

She studied his profile a moment. "Aren't you afraid I'm going to kick your teeth in?"

He blanched. "Who told you that?"

"You did. Next time you wish to insult someone, you might not want to do it in the forest where passersby can hear."

His color rose. "I'm sorry."

"It doesn't matter." She shrugged. "At least we know where we stand."

"I guess we do at that."

From inside her saddlebag, she retrieved two cheese buns and tossed one to Reye.

"Thanks." He took a bite and sighed with pleasure. "That's good. I had to leave so quickly this morning, I didn't have time to pack any food."

"How did you know I'd left?"

"You woke me when you were saddling Myst. I drank too much last night and passed out in the stables."

"Alone?"

He scratched his head. "Well, I…"

"Never mind. I'm sorry I asked."

REYE ATE his way through a large portion of Kira's food supplies, so she was relieved to find a roadside tavern. After watering the horses, they went inside for a midday meal. The burly tavern keeper came over to their table to refill their water mugs.

"I wish I could offer you ice for your drinks but gone are the days when wizards could be counted on for an accommodating spell or two."

"That's all right. It's been such a long time since I've had any ice, I've grown used to it," Kira said.

"I'd give anything for an everlasting orb to light the place at night. My old one petered out last turn and now I'm back to using lanterns," he said. "I'll never get used to life without magic, I'm afraid."

The fellow seemed the friendly type, so Kira seized her chance. "I understand exactly what you mean. A wizard friend of mine disappeared about a turn ago. His name was Dorsit of the Leopard Clan. Did you ever hear anything about it?"

He gave her a look laced with pity. "Lass, 'tis best not to be asking questions about things like that. If your friend is gone, he's either run up against the Wolf Clan wizard or fled to Yrth."

"I don't believe in Yrth," Kira murmured. "But thank you."

The tavern keeper moved on to the next table.

"So this is about Dorsit?" Reye slid her a dubious look. "He's a little old for you, isn't he?"

"No, it's nothing like that. Did you ever meet him?"

"Sure, when he was engaged to your sister. Dorsit was a good fellow, even though he frequently had his head in the clouds."

"He was the elder brother I never had, and a wonderful wizard. My sister might have been changed for the better if she'd married him." Kira averted her gaze. "I just want to know his fate."

"Where are we heading on this quest for knowledge?"

"I thought maybe his friends in Ylan would have heard something."

Reye's eyebrows rose. "That's a long ride from here!"

"You're more than welcome to go home."

"No, no, I'm fine. I'm more scared of Rampen Szul than I am of his daughter. He'd have my head if I let any harm befall you."

Kira paid the tavern keeper for the meal and for extra provisions to replenish what she and Reye had eaten that morning.

"Say…you're not riding east are ye?" the tavern keeper asked.

Reye was purposely vague. "Might be."

"I should warn ye, there've been Cyclopes sightings in the foothills recently."

Kira and Reye exchanged a bewildered glance.

"Did you say the foothills?" Kira asked. "I thought Cyclopes never came down from the mountains."

"I had a fellow come in here yesterday morning who swore

he lost a herd of puledens to a couple of hungry Cyclopes. Poor man was left with nothing."

"Most likely he was playing on your sympathy, trying to get a free meal," Reye said.

"Maybe so, lad, but we wouldn't want anything to happen to your lady friend here. Keep your wits about ye is all I'm saying."

THE TALL TREES on either side of the road made it impossible to see the mountain range in the far distance, but that didn't stop Kira from mulling over what the tavern keeper had told them.

"If the Cyclopes are wandering in Nomad Territory, my father should hear about it."

"Perhaps the tavern keeper has been sampling his own ale," Reye said.

"He seemed sober enough," Kira replied. "Have you ever seen a Cyclops?"

"No, and I can't say I've missed the experience. We don't need to go near the mountains, you know. We could cut across the countryside and head south that way. The terrain might be rugged, but it might be safer."

Kira shook her head. "If Cyclopes are leaving their habitat, I'd like to investigate. My father will want to be informed."

"To confirm a Cyclops sighting, wouldn't we need to be too close for comfort?"

"I'd settle for seeing the tracks."

STRANGE GENTLEMAN

Although Kira wasn't one to complain, seven days on horseback was taking its toll on her muscles. From the way Reye shifted in his saddle from time to time, she guessed she wasn't the only one in discomfort. They were nearly at the southbound fork to Ylan when pain began to shoot up Kira's back and down her thighs. She dismounted her horse, to lead her along by the bridle.

"What's wrong?" Reye asked.

"I've never ridden this long before. I'd almost rather walk to Ylan from here."

Laughing, he dismounted. "I'm glad you're the one to say it first. I was ready to walk beginning yesterday."

She ran her hand down Myst's neck. "Our horses could use a rest, too. There's a well-traveled pass through the mountains at Eastknot Crossing, a few miles from here. I'm certain we'll find an inn with actual beds and a real stable for the horses."

Reye rubbed his behind. "I wouldn't turn down a real bed." He glanced up at the sky, where storm clouds were forming. "I expect Ladies' Man would appreciate a bucket of oats and a dry roof over his head."

"Your stallion is called Ladies' Man?"

"Well, yes. He's named after me."

Kira rolled her eyes and groaned.

Despite their best efforts to reach Eastknot Crossing before the storm hit, Kira and Reye were drenched by the time they arrived. The first inn they encountered was full, but the proprietor directed them to the inn and tavern at the center of town.

"If you've got the gold, Nomads Lodge will probably have rooms for you," she said.

"Thank you," Kira replied.

As they led their horses down the street, Reye groaned.

"I may have to sleep in the stable. I came away from the encampment without much in the way of money."

"My father gave me plenty, I assure you." She shook raindrops from her eyes. "No matter what the cost, it'll be worth it."

As it turned out, Nomads Lodge was quite grand. Although it did not possess the spires and towers of a castle, the building was an imposing two-story structure nonetheless. The spacious stables were equipped with single stalls, and servants were available to tend to their horses. Kira tipped the stable hands well to ensure Myst and Ladies' Man would be groomed, fed, and watered. An unusually fine charger with a shiny black coat was stamping the straw in one of the stalls. Reye was mesmerized.

"What a magnificent steed," he said. "The inn must have an illustrious guest."

"A great many prospectors pass through here, fresh from mining gold in the mountains," she said. "Someone obviously made his fortune."

Reye waved over one of the stablehands. "Rumors have it that Cyclopes have been coming down from the mountains. Have you heard of any sightings around here?"

The boy's face lost its color, and he stared at him, wide-eyed.

Kira jostled Reye with her elbow. "What are you thinking? You've scared the lad out of his wits."

"Sorry, I didn't mean to frighten you," Reye said. "Never mind."

Inside the inn, Kira paid for two rooms and gave Reye his key. The price was steep, but at least meals and baths were included. As she shifted the saddlebags on her shoulder, she noticed he had none. "Have you no change of clothes?"

"I came away only with my weapons and the clothes on my back. Next time you sneak off, you should give me more notice."

She slipped him a gold coin. "Purchase what you need in town. I'll meet you in the tavern for the evening meal."

"Er…I have the feeling things cost a lot more here."

She flipped another gold coin in the air, which he caught handily.

"Thanks."

As he ambled out the door in search of a shop, Kira returned to the tavern keeper's desk.

"I'd like to have a bath. Could you send someone to my room with hot water?"

"No need for that, lass. The bathtub is enchanted."

"You've a wizard on staff?"

"Aye, a Turtle Clan wizard by the name of Patnik."

"I'd like to speak with him while I'm here."

"We have many important people who stay with us, and he can't be bothered to see every single person who asks."

Kira slid a gold coin across the desk, and lowered her voice. "Tell him Nomad Chief Rampen Szul's daughter requests a meeting."

The tavern keeper's jaw dropped. "Why didn't you say so! I'll send for him immediately."

"Not now. I've been traveling, and I need to clean off the dust."

As she turned away from the desk, the tavern keeper

hastened after her. He introduced himself as Zed and insisted on carrying her bags up the stairs to her room. Weary and saddle sore, she accepted his help. Inside her room, he demonstrated how the cast-iron tub automatically filled with water when occupied, and how the temperature of the water could be controlled by way of red or blue stones set in the wall.

When she was alone, she wasted no time settling into the tub to soak. Rain drummed against her windows and she was grateful for a roof over her head. As she relaxed, she wondered if Patnik could tell her anything about Dorsit. The Turtle Clan wizard couldn't be too powerful if he'd escaped Efysian's notice…particularly not when Eastknot Crossing was almost in Wolf Mountain's shadow. Nevertheless, his magical ability was less important than whether or not he could tell her anything about Dorsit's fate.

Kira dressed for the evening meal in a fresh pair of breeches and a violet tunic. Kysandra had given the tunic to her on her last birthday, but she'd never worn the feminine garment until now. To her delight, an enchanted boot rack in the closet had also magically cleaned and polished her boots while she was bathing.

When Kira descended the stairs, she noticed an older gentleman chatting with Zed in the entryway. She knew the man was a wizard by the silvery transporter cuff on his wrist and the clan ring on his finger. The tavern keeper beckoned her over.

"This is Patnik of the Turtle Clan, Princess," Zed said. "I've told him you have some questions." He bustled off.

"How may I be of service?" the wizard asked.

"I'm seeking information about a Leopard Clan wizard by the name of Dorsit. He disappeared less than a turn ago, somewhere between Wyckcrest and Ylan. I was wondering if you'd ever heard any news of him?"

The man frowned and shook his head. "I know nothing

specific, but if he disappeared suddenly, I can only imagine he tangled with the Wolf Clan wizard."

Disappointment washed over her. "You'd think if Efysian was killing all the wizards, their remains would be found sooner or later."

"I heard a rumor that Efysian keeps a hungry wolf in his lair."

Kira recoiled at the implication. "*Good Solegra*, I hope that's not it!"

"I wish I could be of more help. Was there anything else?"

"Yes…have there been any Cyclopes seen around here?"

The wizard blanched. "What a thing to ask! It would be difficult to keep a thing like that secret, wouldn't it?" His laugh sounded forced. "Tell your father he has nothing at all to worry about on that score."

Patnik jumped to his feet and hastened out the door, leaving a bewildered Kira staring after him. The wizard's response to her last question was peculiar, to say the least. He'd been unnerved, certainly, and almost evasive in his reply. Was he hiding something, or was he just unsettled by the mention of Cyclopes?

When she entered the dining room and glanced around for a place to sit, she noticed Reye had returned from his shopping excursion bedecked with a foppish shirt and new breeches. He was chatting at the bar with an extraordinarily good-looking man, whose smooth, long black hair was held back from his elegant face by a leather tie. She noticed his eyes were lined with kohl. Although she'd never seen such a thing before on a man, she had to admit the affectation was very attractive. His appearance excited a pleasant sort of heat at her center, and she wondered if Reye planned to introduce him.

She took a corner table, and shortly thereafter Reye joined her. To her pleasure, he'd brought the stranger along. Taller even than Reye, the man was athletic, with sleek powerful muscles seemingly coiled to strike. The planes of his face were angular, throwing his broad cheekbones in stark relief. Again, she felt a fluttering sensation at her core that sent a warm flush across her body. She was undeniably attracted to him—and him to her if the slight smile on his lips was any indication.

"Kira, this is Mandral," Reye said. "He's a fellow traveler and a charming fellow. I've asked him to join us for dinner."

"If it's not too much of an imposition," Mandral added.

His silky voice sent shockwaves down her spine and her mouth went dry. "Not at all," she managed. "I'm sure Reye and I would love to hear stories of your travels."

They ordered a meal from a serving girl who could not seem to decide if she preferred Reye or Mandral. After the girl deposited mugs of ale on the table, Reye proposed a toast.

"To fellow travelers."

As Kira sipped her ale, her eyes met Mandral's and she wished his presence wasn't so distracting. Reye put his mug down with a sigh of satisfaction.

"It's been a long time since I've had anything this cold to drink."

"The lodge employs a wizard, hadn't you noticed?" Kira said. "There are several wonderful enchantments in my room."

"Wizards can be exceedingly full of themselves, but they have their uses," Mandral said.

A giggle escaped Kira's lips, which annoyed her. Mandral might be the first attractive man she'd met outside Wyckcrest Village, but she needn't turn into a simpering fool.

"Our new friend here just rode over the mountain pass," Reye said. "I told him you're my sister, and we're visiting relatives to the south."

Reye's cover story was unexpectedly cautious, but Kira welcomed it. Mandral was handsome and well-spoken, but they knew nothing about him. In fact, she wished she'd been more circumspect with Zed and Patnik.

"Where are you from, originally?" she asked.

"A small northeast Territory nobody ever heard of." Mandral waved his hand dismissively. "I thought I would explore the continent a bit to see if there was someplace I liked better."

"I've only ever traveled to Gnoam Territory, but Nomad Territory is unparalleled, in my opinion," she said. "Our soil produces rich crops and the people are hard-working."

"And Nomad Territory is home to uncommonly attractive women," Mandral said.

Her flush grew warmer.

"Er…Reye and I heard a rumor that Cyclopes were stirring from their habitat high up in the mountains," she said. "Did you happen to see the creatures when you came through the pass?"

His well-defined eyebrows lifted. "Not one. I believe someone must have been joking with you."

Kira exchanged a glance with Reye, who shrugged.

"I suppose it's possible," he said.

"I hope so," she replied. "Tell me, Mandral, do you know of any wizards still living east of the mountains?"

"A few purveyors of charms still roam from town to town, hawking their wares," he replied. "What about in Nomad Territory?"

"The wizard working at Nomads Lodge is the first one I've encountered in almost a turn," Kira said.

"Efysian of the Wolf Clan has pretty much wiped them all out," Reye said.

"It will be fascinating to see how the lack of magic affects the balance of world power going forward," Mandral said. "Without wizardry, warlords will have to rely on armies to make their conquests."

"I sense you have an interest in politics?" Kira asked.

"I have many interests, including politics and alchemy."

Kira's interest was sparked. "Alchemy? I've an interest in

mixing essential oils, but mainly to blend of fragrances and soap."

"That accounts for your intoxicating aroma of lilac," he said.

"I'm flattered you noticed."

Reye cleared his throat. "That's a beautiful blade by your side. I expect you know how to use it."

"Ah, yes. I'd like to think of myself as a capable swordsman," Mandral said. "Undoubtedly I'm no equal to a Nomad warrior. Their combat skills are superior, so I'm told."

"I've heard that too." She sipped her ale to cover her mirth.

When her meal arrived, she was surprised at her ravenous appetite. She devoted her attention to the thick slice of roast puleden set before her and to the myriad of side dishes. Certainly if Kysandra were watching, she'd rebuke her for eating so much. She gave Mandral an apologetic glance.

"Forgive me, but I haven't been this hungry in a long while."

"The road sometimes whets the appetite. That, and pleasant company."

Reye said nothing because his mouth was full. After a few minutes, Mandral twisted around in his seat, glancing around the busy tavern.

"Is something amiss?" Kira asked.

"Only that you and I need more ale, and our server is busy." He rose and picked up his mug along with hers. "I'll have them refilled at the bar."

"Thank you."

Mandral pushed his way through the crowd with the mugs held aloft. Kira gave Reye a pointed glance. "He's quite a gentleman, unlike some people I know."

Feigned hurt. "I can be a gentleman."

"You've trailed your lace in the gravy."

"Blazes!" Reye promptly stuck the stained fabric in his mouth.

"If the rain has stopped, I think we should depart after breakfast tomorrow."

He snickered. "I had the impression you wished to tarry."

"Unlike you, I'm not in the habit of tarrying with attractive strangers. Besides which, my father would have a fit if he knew I was talking with him."

Mandral returned with the ale. Although Kira hadn't been particularly fond of the flavor at first, it seemed to grow on her the longer she sipped it. *Perhaps it's the ice.* She gulped the ale down, wiped the foam from her upper lip, and gave Mandral a grateful smile.

"This is delicious."

Their eyes locked and she had no wish to look away. The man was a miracle of male beauty so exquisite, Kira was amazed he existed at all. Nothing else mattered except for Mandral. *I'm nothing without him.*

"Kira, are you all right?" Reye asked. "You seem lost in your thoughts."

She was annoyed at the interruption. *Why can't he go away and leave us alone?* "Never better."

Reye peered at her. "Perhaps you should turn in and get some rest. We're setting off early tomorrow."

Panic gripped her. "So soon? Surely not."

Even as she spoke, she realized something wasn't right. *Not five minutes ago I told Reye we would ride for Ylan tomorrow morning and now I can't bear the thought of never seeing Mandral again.*

Confused, she stood. "I think I'll retire after all."

The gentlemen rose too. Mandral's half-lidded eyes caressed her face and body and her confusion lifted. *I love him.*

He brought her trembling hand to his lips. "Sleep well."

His words were plain enough, but she knew he really meant he loved her more passionately than any man had ever loved a woman throughout all eternity. A single tear of happiness found its way down her cheek. *I love him so dearly!* With Reye listening, however, she could not tell Mandral exactly how much she adored him, body and soul.

"Let me see you to your room," Mandral said.

His hand slid around her elbow, and she melted at his touch. As they walked through the tavern, she could not tear her eyes away from his handsome profile. His nearness sent an intoxicating sensation through her veins, and she found it difficult to catch her breath. When they mounted the stairs together, his arm snaked around her waist and she leaned into him.

"I love you," she said.

"I know. Swear you'll marry me on your word as a Nomad."

"Oh, yes. You have my word."

Outside her door, he kissed her over and over again in a rough, demanding way that made her heart pound.

"I will come to you tonight if my business concludes early," he murmured.

"I can't wait."

Her heart broke as he walked away down the hall, even though a small voice in her head told her the events of the evening had unfolded in a peculiar manner. *I'm so in love with the man...and yet how is that possible?* Her longing was so desperate and intense, it took all her will power not to run after him and beg him to stay. *Clear your head and think!* Kira entered her room, and as she stared at her panting, glassy-eyed reflection in the mirror, she froze with a sudden realization.

I've been poisoned.

THE GAME BEGINS

From Zed, Kira obtained directions to the nearest apothecary. As the apothecary mixed up an emetic for her, he gave her a worried glance.

"Is everything as it should be, lass?"

She forced herself to nod and smile. "I've a stomachache. Please hurry."

He paused his grinding. "A simple peppermint draught would be more effective."

An extra silver coin caused the apothecary to redouble his efforts. With a quick word of thanks, Kira grabbed the bottle and emerged onto the boardwalk lining one side of the street. Darkness had long since fallen and clouds overhead blotted out most of the moonlight. Turning down a muddy alley, she darted into a copse of trees and drank the contents of the bottle in one go. Almost as soon as she swallowed the fluid, her stomach expelled everything she had eaten or drank at dinner…and then some.

Shaky and ill, Kira leaned against a tree and tried to recover her composure. Moisture from the recent rain dripped from leaves overhead, rolling down her face like tears. As she lurched back toward the main street, mud squelched underneath her boots with a sucking sound and she almost lost her footing several times. Without a doubt, Mandral had slipped a love potion in her ale at dinner, but what had he hoped to gain? A man as handsome as Mandral could easily obtain willing female companionship without resorting to trickery. Embarrassment and shame made her skin crawl when she remembered how she'd positively *fawned* over him at dinner and let him kiss her afterward. She'd even promised to marry him!

As fury at Mandral's treachery erupted within her, however, it was accompanied by a pathetic, gnawing hunger to see him again. Although the giddiness she'd felt earlier had dissipated, an irrational obsession remained. *It's not real. The remaining effects of the poison will wear off by morning, surely, and I must maintain control of myself until then.* Her footsteps paused. *When he comes to my room tonight, I won't be able to resist. I must keep away from the lodge until I'm sure he has given me up as a lost cause.*

She veered into the stables, slipping unnoticed past a group of stable boys playing cards in the corner. Myst nickered when Kira entered her stall. As she stroked the mare's flank, she noted with approval the horse had been brushed and groomed properly and was supplied with fresh oats and water. *One of us, at least, is happy.* Abundant clean straw covered the floor, and she made herself comfortable next to the water trough. When a small white newtic scurried across the toe of her boot, Kira forced herself not to flinch. She'd never been afraid of the silly rodents, but they made a loud popping noise when touched. Should the stable boys hear the sound, they might come investigate. *Imagine their surprise when they discover a cowering Nomad princess writhing in the throes of love sickness.*

～

MURMURING VOICES WOKE Kira from an uneasy sleep. A sharp pain in her neck made her wince, and she cursed the circumstances keeping her from the comfortable bed she'd paid for. *It must be late…perhaps my virtue will be safe now and I can return to my room.* She dragged herself upright and stretched, but immediately ducked behind a pillar when she realized she wasn't alone. Mandral was leading the huge black charger from its stall several yards away, while Patnik waited near the stable entrance.

"The current threat has been neutralized," Mandral said. "It's time to execute my plan."

Delicious shivers went down Kira's spine at the sound of the man's sensual voice. Her eyes closed and she longed to touch his hand and feel the warmth of his smile. In the next moment, she shook herself. *These feelings aren't real. Stay hidden and don't move!*

"The wizard Dorsit has been seen in Ylan, Warlord. If the Nomads seek his help, he may present a complication. I advise you to tie up the loose ends immediately."

Dorsit is alive? And Patnik called Mandral a warlord!

Mandral chuckled. "I don't want her harmed. The girl is under my thrall, and the idea of marriage to the Nomad Chief's daughter rather pleases me. It's been many turns since I've seen such a comely wench."

He knew who I was all along.

"With Kira by my side, the Nomads will more readily accept a coup," Mandral said.

"Why don't you poison the Nomads the same way you poisoned the princess?"

"Alas, I used the last of the love potion on the girl. Until the passion flowers bloom again next spring, I can't brew more. It's of little consequence. I've paid the barmaid to slit her bodyguard's throat come morning, and Kira shall ride with me to her father's encampment as my future bride."

"With your permission, I'll transport directly to the base camp. Captain Blane is awaiting your orders."

"Tell him to send squads of cygards to surround Eastknot Crossing immediately. Nobody is permitted in or out. I'll meet you at the base camp to review the rest of my troops personally. At first light, the game begins."

Mandral spurred his horse forward. As the warlord rode from the stable, Patnik transported away in a flash of light and low boom of thunder. Kira let out the breath she'd been holding. *Oh, Solegra! Nomad Territory is being invaded!*

AS QUIETLY AS POSSIBLE, Kira turned the key in the lock and swung Reye's door open. The warrior and his bed partner had fallen asleep and were tangled up in the sheets. Kira closed the door and fumbled for the latch on the everlasting orb lantern overhead. As illumination filled the room, Reye finally stirred. "Is it daylight already?"

The barmaid woke, gasping as she felt the tip of Kira's sword hovering under her chin.

"Get dressed," Kira demanded. "Scream and I'll kill you."

The woman hurried to comply as Reye raised himself on one elbow. "Why are you here and how in blazes did you get a key to my room?"

"I stole it from Zed. If you want your companion here to live, tie her up and gag her."

"What?"

"I don't have time to explain. Just do it or I'll let her slit your throat like she'd planned."

"Treena? She wouldn't have—"

The barmaid suddenly whirled around, a long stiletto in her hand. Without batting an eye, Kira used the flat of her sword to knock the weapon to one side.

"I guess I spoke too soon," Reye muttered.

He tied Treena to the bed, stuck a wadded pillowcase in her mouth, and turned toward Kira. "So what's going on?"

"I'll tell you later. Hurry up and get dressed. We're leaving."

Clad in his underwear, Reye gestured for Kira to turn around. "D'you mind?"

A few minutes later, the two Nomads crept from the room. Since it was the dead of night, nobody was stirring.

"What's this all about?" he whispered.

"Shh!" She paused to listen. "Do you hear that?"

He cocked his head. In the distance, the faint sound of clanking metal was barely audible.

"Is that a thunderstorm?"

Fear drained the blood from her face. "No. It's much worse."

With her sword still drawn, she led the way downstairs. Through the open doors of the adjoining tavern, she noticed a few men hunched over mugs of ale. None were sober enough to be a threat, so Kira and Reye crept past undetected.

When they emerged from the lodge, he yanked her down behind a horse trough in time to escape the notice of a squad of armor-clad Cyclopes marching south down the main street. Huge axes and other weapons hung from the giants' belts or were gripped in their massive fists.

"What on Yden are those creatures?" Reye whispered.

"Mandral calls them cygards," she murmured. "He's formed an army of Cyclopes."

"That's insane!"

"If we don't get out of Eastknot before his cygards surround the town, we'll be captured. My father will have no warning what's about to befall Nomad Territory."

"Wyckcrest is seven days from here," Reye said. "Even if we rode hard, we wouldn't get there in time to do much good."

"Ylan is four days away, and I just learned Dorsit is alive. He can transport us directly to my father's encampment and help us fight off the invasion. I fear he's our only hope."

Reye nodded, peeked over the trough to make sure no cygards were watching, and then pulled Kira to her feet.

"Let's move."

~

WHEN REYE and Kira crept into the stable, they gasped with dismay at the sight of the four stable boys lying in a bloody heap with their throats cut.

"Why would anyone kill children?" Reye exclaimed.

"I suspect Mandral had cygards kill them for knowing too much."

An expression of incredulity passed over his face. "And to think I actually *liked* that fellow."

And to think I actually love him. No, not love. Whatever I feel, it's not that.

"We should stay off the main roads on our way out of town," she said. "Fortunately, cygards tend to make a racket with their armor. Hopefully, we can avoid them."

Under the cover of darkness, Kira and Reye rode south, zigzagging through alleys and cutting across the swaths of forest surrounding Eastknot. When they reached the squads of cygards fanned out along the southern perimeter of the town, they were forced to detour east into the foothills to avoid detection. Unfortunately, they were in the center of an open field when Solegra sent glimmers of light radiating across Yden. Cygards spotted them immediately and began to close in. Reye drew his sword.

"You go on, Kira. I'll lead them away."

"I can't let you do that!"

"This isn't about you or me, it's about Nomad Territory. Ride for Ylan and find a way to warn your father. I fear it's already too late."

Without another word, Reye spurred his horse into a westerly gallop, and Kira was left with no choice but to urge Myst into a flat run around the cygards' flank. When they realized she was about to escape, a pair of cygards tried to intercept her. She was shocked at how fast the huge creatures could move, even weighed down by heavy armor.

At the far side of the field, Myst jumped over the four-foot-high zigzag fence. To Kira's horror, the first cygard plowed right through the fence, sending splintered wood flying. Thereafter he tripped over one of the scattered logs and fell with a crash. The second cygard tried to hurtle the debris, but he too was felled by a log. Cygards weren't too bright, she concluded, and once they'd fallen, getting up was problematic for them. She had no further opportunities to make observations, however, because the open road to Ylan lay ahead and she didn't look back.

Pressing south over the next few days, Kira spared neither herself nor her horse. After Myst tired, Kira dismounted and led her by the bridle until she herself couldn't take another step. Fortunately the road was parallel to the river, so water was plentiful. With no food supplies with her, and no settlements between Eastknot and Ylan, Kira was forced to hunt. It didn't improve her temper when several freshwater nymphs laughed at her attempts to spear fish in the river with a stiletto. Her ability with throwing knives enabled her to secure rabbits, which she cooked along with some tubers she found growing in the shallows.

At night, her scant few hours' sleep were interrupted by tortured dreams of Mandral and their hopeless love. After she woke with tears of longing on her face, she began to realize the poison wasn't wearing off. The emetic she'd used may have taken the edge off the obsession, but her feelings for the man were like a constant ache or a festering wound. If any good had come from her predicament, she now knew what love was *not*. True love would make her happy, not miserable. She would feel strong, not weak. The purity of love should lift her higher, but instead she felt dirty inside.

On those occasions when she managed to push Mandral from her mind, Kira worried about Reye. Had he managed to escape capture? If not, his chances for survival were slim. Those poor, murdered stable boys were proof of Mandral's ruthlessness, if any additional proof was necessary. Whenever she thought about Reye's sacrifice, she was determined not to let it go to waste.

When Kira reached Ylan, she was bedraggled and reeling from emotional and physical exhaustion. Although the village was picturesque and brimming with Dorsit's magical touches, she wasn't interested in sightseeing. She rode Myst into the first stable she could find, and insisted on removing the mare's saddle and bridle personally. An attendant carried buckets of water and oats into the stall, and while the horse ate, Kira rested her forehead against the mare's neck and murmured her thanks.

Towel in one hand and grooming brush in the other, the attendant began to rub Myst down.

"I'm looking for someone," Kira said. "Do you know where Dorsit of the Leopard Clan lives?"

The attendant gave a barking sort of laugh. "I'm not sure he does, exactly."

In no mood for cryptic jokes, Kira bit back a sharp retort.

"Look, can you just tell me where to find him? It's critically important."

"He's got a room at the Two Moon Inn. Ask for Emberr, the owner."

"Thank you."

Her muscles shaking from fatigue, Kira picked up her saddlebags, left the stable, and headed into town. The large central plaza was full of life and movement, as children played next to fanciful, posing topiary and a color-changing fountain in the late afternoon suns. When Kira spied the leopard statue in the center of the fountain, tears stung her eyes. The plaza and everything in it was Dorsit's handiwork. Whatever reason he'd had for staying away so long didn't matter. She was certain the wizard would help her father repel an invasion if she asked him.

The Two Moon Inn—identifiable from its wooden hanging sign—was not too far from the plaza. Despite her exhaustion, her pace quickened. Dorsit could transport her home in minutes, and there wasn't a moment to lose. The entrance of the inn led directly into a large, open tavern, with several long wooden tables in the middle, and several smaller round ones in the corners. Although she'd expected the room to be dimly lit, the room was illuminated by a decorative series of everlasting orbs encased in attractive lanterns attached to the walls like sconces. The dinner crowd had not yet arrived, but a few men were chatting and drinking ice-cold mugs of ale at one of the long tables. An extremely elderly man with long white hair sat in the corner, drawing pictures on a parchment. He glanced up when Kira appeared, and she couldn't repress a shudder at the fixed stare radiating from his sunken sockets. The poor fellow obviously had one foot in the grave.

A buxom woman with a pretty face stepped out from around the bar. "Can I help you, lass? Might you be needing a room?"

"Yes." Kira lowered her saddlebags into a nearby chair. "Are you Emberr?"

"That I am."

"I was told Dorsit of the Leopard Clan was staying here."

"Aye, he's sitting over there." Emberr nodded toward the elderly fellow in the corner.

"No, I'm looking for a young Leopard Clan wizard."

"And you've found him," Emberr said. "Mind you don't get him over excited. He's not in the best of health these days."

The elderly man had risen from his table and hobbled closer. "Kira Szul? You've grown up so much I almost didn't know you."

As she recognized Dorsit's voice, Kira gasped and turned. She peered into his face and saw the truth in his eyes...just before she blacked out.

ENEMY WITHIN

Fog whirled all around Kira's body, spectral and yet with eerie substance. In the distance, Mandral called to her, his arms open in invitation. His deep-timbered voice kindled a desperate yearning within and she couldn't wait to join him. She darted forward, but white tendrils gripped her arms and legs, holding her fast. Mandral gave her a sad smile, and as he turned to walk away, she screamed in heart-broken agony…

Kira swam to consciousness, waking with a sobbing cry. Although her berth was soft and comfortable, her head throbbed and she felt nauseous. A rough bony hand crept into hers, and she turned to see who was attempting to comfort her. She was startled to discover the elderly man from the tavern sitting in a chair at her bedside. Her eyes fell to the Leopard Clan ring on his finger and she blanched. No, not just any elderly man—*Dorsit!*

Sitting up proved to be impossible.

"What's wrong with me?" she managed.

"You hit your head when you lost consciousness," Dorsit said. "You must lay still."

She examined his face more closely. Now that she knew who he was, she recognized a few distinctive features. Dorsit's eyes were still the deepest marine blue, his snowy hair—formerly raven—still hung to his waist, his teeth were straight and white, and his clothes were as elegant as ever. His handsome looks were long gone, however, and despite her best efforts not to cry, fat tears crept from her eyes and moistened her pillow.

"Oh, Dorsit, what happened to you?"

"Efysian captured me, as you may have guessed."

"Why?"

"The Wolf Clan wizard has been sustaining himself on wizards' life energy. When he thought me dead, he released me from the spell holding me captive. The Guardian of his lair took pity on me, I suppose, because she helped me escape from his cavern in Wolf Mountain. Unfortunately, I'm now drained."

"What does that mean?"

"I can only perform the most minor sorts of magic now, and only then when I am well-rested and fed. The last significant thing I accomplished was transporting to Ylan from Wolf Mountain. Some of the townspeople found me unconscious in the street and brought me to Emberr. I've been slowly getting my strength back since."

"How can we restore you completely?"

"We can't. A few herbs sustain me somewhat, but there is no way to renew my life energy." His smile was sad. "Considering the alternative, however, things aren't all bad. The Guardian told me I'm the only wizard ever to have escaped with my life."

Despite the pain in her skull, Kira suddenly remembered why she'd come.

"Dorsit, can you transport me to Wyckcrest?"

"Alas, such magic is still beyond me."

Kira gritted her teeth and made a noise of frustration. "A warlord from the east is staging an invasion of Nomad Territory."

"What?"

"Mandral has recruited the Cyclopes as an army, and Patnik of the Turtle Clan as an ally. They are marching to Wyckcrest even now, and I must warn my father."

"You've seen this for yourself?"

She nodded. "Only Reye's heroic actions allowed me to escape Eastknot Village so I might seek your help."

Dorsit's white eyebrows drew together. "I believe I can conjure a courier bird to carry your message to Rampen Szul."

"Please do it as soon as you can. Dorsit, the cygards saw me ride south. Ylan will not be safe now—for the residents or for us."

He stood. "I'll direct the mayor to put the town on alert."

After he left, despair descended. As formidable and fearsome as Nomad warriors were, her father could not hope to repel the invasion with only a few days' preparation. Casualties would be horrendous...and then what? The ruthless, devious warlord would claim Nomad Territory as his own, and the aftermath would be a reign of terror.

And yet I long to see Mandral's face again.

KIRA WROTE a letter to her father, and Dorsit successfully conjured a courier bird to deliver it. He also summoned a local healer named Adrea to examine Kira in her room. The woman tsked over the black and blue lump on her forehead and prepared a suitable poultice from the herbs in her travel case. As she worked, Kira blurted out the question that had been burning on her tongue.

"Do you know anything about love potions?"

Adrea's eyebrows lifted. "They're illegal in every civilized territory."

"M-My sister joked about using one once. I discouraged her, but afterward I was curious if such a thing works."

"Well…a love potion doesn't produce actual love, if that's what you mean. It's more of a permanent addiction, and quite an excruciating one too, I'm told."

"But there's an antidote, isn't there?"

"Not of which I am aware. In fact, such potions can drive people mad with longing over time."

Kira's heart sank. Adrea soaked a linen bandage in the poultice mixture and arranged it over her injury. The pain lessened immediately, and she was able to focus her thoughts.

"That feels much better, thank you."

Adrea smiled. "I wish it were that easy to treat love potion poisoning. The only thing that lessens the craving is complete lack of contact with the poisoner." A chuckle escaped her lips. "There's an old wives' tale about love potions, but I don't put any faith in it."

"Tell me."

"They say the potion's spell can only be broken when you meet your true love." A shrug. "It's romantic nonsense, of course."

As the healer prepared to leave, Kira caught her hand. "Is there truly nothing to be done for Dorsit?"

"I'm doing what I can, lass, but his strength comes and goes. A tea made of the grail mushroom might prove beneficial, but none grow around here."

"There's a field of them quite close to Wyckcrest. I never realized they had medicinal properties."

Although Kira tried to give Adrea money for her services, the healer declined to take it.

"Dorsit paid me already. You rest now. The headache will continue to improve, but you'll have a bruise for a few days."

After the healer was gone, Kira lay in bed and stared up at the ceiling. As she'd feared, her emotional misery was permanent and her shame complete. The only recourse was to avoid Mandral forever and to somehow meet her true love. Mirthless laughter bubbled to her lips since neither possibility seemed likely. *I'm a warrior and the only thing a warrior knows how to do is fight. Only now I'm fighting an enemy within, and I can't afford to lose.*

THE FOLLOWING MORNING, Kira rose from her bed feeling a great deal better. Adrea's poultice had removed the pain and swelling on her forehead, and a long bath helped restore her sense of dignity. Like the Eastknot Lodge, the Two Moon Inn had magical bathrooms. Here, however, the temperature controls were activated by dual moon symbols over the floating spigot. Because she was out of fresh clothes, Emberr loaned her a gown until her things could be laundered. The garment was far too large, but Kira was in no position to complain.

After Kira dressed, she joined Dorsit in the tavern for breakfast.

"Any news from my father?" she asked.

"Not yet. Mayor Pool has positioned two men to act as sentries at the north end of town. If they spot anything threatening heading this way, we'll hear the alarm."

"We can't stay here, Dorsit. Mandral knows who I am. If I'm captured, he'll try to use me against my father. He'll also try to kill you."

"Why me? I'm no menace to anyone."

"To prevent you from using magic to repel the invasion, of course."

"I can't. Not any longer."

"He'll still view you as a threat. You're in as much danger as I am."

Emberr served them egg and cheese pie, thick slices of

bacon, and biscuits with jam. When she saw and smelled the food, Kira's mouth watered.

"You look as if you haven't eaten in days, and you're far too thin," Dorsit said.

"Fleeing from cygards tends to do that to a girl. Beside, you're one to talk; you're as slender as a nymph's virtue."

A flicker of his former spark showed in his eyes. "I suppose you have me there."

They both set their attention to the meal, and only after the Leopard Clan wizard had urged her to eat a third biscuit did her stomach rebel.

"I can't eat another bite."

He folded his napkin and put it on the table. "You've not said a word about Kysandra. I presume, therefore, you've no good tidings for me."

"I expect she's married to Warlord Laramy and on her way to his territory by now."

His gaze dropped to the table. "Thank you for your honesty. I'm glad for her, since there is no way I could have hoped to make a proper bridegroom."

"Kysandra wasn't worthy of you, Dorsit." She covered his hand with hers. "No matter what happens, I won't rest until I discover a cure for your condition."

And for mine.

"Good Solegra!" Rampen Szul's hand shook as he read his daughter's letter. A magical courier bird the color of Kira's violet eyes perched on the table, awaiting his written reply. In the next moment, Szul sounded a bell to draw his most elite warriors and captains into a conclave. While he waited, he scribbled instructions to his daughter on a parchment, rolled it thin, and tied it to the bird's leg. The creature flew from the tent, followed closely by Szul. He summoned a team of scouts and instructed them to ride east.

"Whatever you may see, don't engage the enemy. Return as swiftly as possible to give me your report."

The scouts raced toward the stables, just as a bewildered conclave assembled underneath the pavilion where the nuptials of the Nomad chief's eldest daughter had taken place the week before. When Szul read Kira's letter aloud, the information contained therein was met with incredulity.

"This is madness! Cyclopes don't come down from the mountains!"

"It's inconceivable that an unknown warlord would invade Nomad Territory."

"I've never heard of this Mandral, nor of a Turtle Clan wizard named Patnik."

"Forgive me, but isn't possible this message is a young girl's prank, meant to sow panic as revenge for being sent away?"

Szul scowled. "My daughter would never make up lies to inconvenience the Nomads! Furthermore, she would not have involved Dorsit of the Leopard Clan in her deceit."

"If Dorsit lives, why didn't he bring the message himself? The Leopard Clan wizard is a powerful ally. With his help, the Nomads can repel any invaders."

The Nomad chief brandished the parchment. "Kira writes that Dorsit has suffered grave injuries at the hands of Efysian and is only a shade of his former self. He can render little aid."

The conclave fell silent as the gravity of the situation finally sunk in. Szul scanned the faces of his warriors. "Prepare for war."

As the day wore on, Kira became increasingly anxious. She donned her freshly laundered clothes, strapped on her sword belt, and went to find Dorsit. The wizard sat in the Central Plaza, sunning himself like a cat. He opened his eyes when she sat next to him on the bench.

"After being held in a cavern for months, I can't seem to get enough sunlight."

"Dorsit, we can stay here no longer. My father's reply will just have to find us on the road."

His response was interrupted by the a warning bell ringing at the north end of town. Without waiting for Dorsit, Kira bolted toward the alarm. At the same time, the citizens of Ylan poured out of their homes and shops, carrying whatever items they could use for defensive purposes.

The alarm bell was coming from a church steeple. Kira burst into the building and leaped up the winding stair to the bell tower, where several townspeople had volunteered as sentries. To the north, dust from the road formed a faint cloud on the horizon. The mayor had a spyglass trained on the cloud, and his expression was incredulous.

"I don't understand what I'm seeing," he said. "Metal giants are coming this way."

When Kira peered through the spyglass, her blood ran cold. Four squads of fully armed cygards were approaching the town at a shuffling run. Their heavy weapons were no match for the citizens of Ylan, who had armed themselves with broomsticks, scythes, and pitchforks.

"They aren't metal giants, they're cygards—Cyclops in armor," she said. "You must stand down or your people will be slaughtered."

Mayor Pool gave her a look of disgust. "This coming from a supposed Nomad warrior?"

A stab of annoyance made Kira grit her teeth.

"You've no idea what you're dealing with, and only a fool would attempt to defeat an overwhelming force with inferior weapons! If you surrender without a struggle, the bulk of the cygards will move on. Then, and only then, will you be able to mount resistance with the ones remaining."

"Makes sense, Mayor," the blacksmith chimed in.

"Cygards have two weaknesses," she said. "First, their armor is too heavy. When they've fallen over, they have a difficult time getting up again...like a turtle on its back. Second, there is a small gap between the helmet and the gorget around their neck. Once a cygard is down, a broadax or sword will separate his head from his shoulders quite nicely."

The mayor listened, albeit grudgingly. "What happens when this warlord discovers the cygards are missing?"

"By then we'll know which way the war is going. If my father can't blunt the invasion, Nomad Territory will fall. If that's the case, we'll have more to worry about than a few dead cygards."

"It's too bad Dorsit is so useless now." The blacksmith was a massive man, but he blanched when he realized the Leopard Clan wizard had appeared. "Er...no offense, wizard."

A wave of sympathy swept over Kira at Dorsit's wounded expression. His chest heaved from climbing the stairs, and his wrinkled skin was covered with a fine sheen of perspiration.

"None taken, Wenx. You're right to say I can do very little to help anymore." He handed Kira a rolled parchment. "This just came for you."

Her hands shook as she unrolled the message and read the contents.

"My father is assessing the situation and preparing to mobilize. He's ordered me to stay in Ylan for now." She laughed, mirthlessly. "No doubt he believed Ylan was safe."

Dorsit frowned suddenly and cocked his head. "Do you hear that?"

Although she listened, only the sound of distant clanking armor reached her ears.

"I hear cygards, which isn't unexpected given the—"

"No, there's something else...like baying dogs." Dorsit

reached for the spyglass and trained it on the rapidly approaching dust cloud. A soft gasp came from his thin lips.

"Patnik must have conjured shadow hounds!"

"Shadow hounds?" the blacksmith exclaimed. "If this is an invasion, who are they tracking?"

Kira gripped the railing. "Me. And if that's the case, maybe I can save Ylan after all."

QUARRY

Kira saddled Myst while Dorsit hovered nearby.

"I just hope this ploy succeeds," she said. "The residents of Ylan deserve better than to be slaughtered."

"You're not going to give yourself up, are you?" The wizard's fists were clenched, as if he planned to stop her.

"Not without a fight. I'll head north out of town, and then ride west across the open countryside. If they follow my scent, I'll lead them away from Ylan. If not, well, the mayor knows what to do."

"Where will you go?"

"With shadow hounds tracking me, I can't go to my cousins' home in Cheernaught like I'd planned." Kira shrugged and gave Dorsit a crooked smile. "I suppose I'll figure it out. I'm a Nomad after all. We're supposed to wander."

"How on Yden does Mandral even know who you are?"

Kira pretended to adjust her stirrup. "I-I…met him in East-knot. Reye and I dined with him before we knew what he intended." She gulped. "He can be very disarming."

A young lad came running into the stables carrying Kira's saddlebags and the borrowed gown she'd worn earlier.

"Here you are, Princess," he said, gasping for breath. "Everything was exactly where you said it would be."

She ruffled his hair and paid him with one of her coins. "Now go home and don't come out until your mother or father tells you it's okay."

"Aye, and good luck!" The boy darted off.

"Please apologize to Emberr for my taking this dress," Kira said to Dorsit. "I hope to toss it down a cliff if the opportunity presents itself. The scent might confuse the hounds, and perhaps the cygards will take me for dead."

"Ride west five miles, then head south until you reach the cliffs at Ylan Bay. After you get rid of the dress, go east along the shore until you reach the fisherman's village. I'll be waiting for you at the pier."

"What are you planning?"

"I'm going to hire a fishing vessel to ferry us and our horses to Gallina Point on the west side of the bay. I'll be surprised if the shadow hounds can swim that far."

"A bold plan, but I don't know if I have enough gold left to execute it."

"I've got plenty of treasure, I assure you. I'll explain when we've set sail."

Kira threw her arms around Dorsit, being careful not to crush his frail bones. "If I don't see you again, I want you to know I'm glad you're alive."

He kissed her forehead "You'll make it, Kira. You're a survivor."

EMBERR LOOKED on in disapproval as Dorsit packed clothes and a few necessities in a knapsack.

"Your little friend nearly brought disaster on this town, just by coming here," she said.

"Ylan is safe, for now. The shadow hounds and cygards are following her scent west."

"The metal giants might return."

"If so, it won't have anything to do with Kira. Nomad Territory is at war."

"I still don't understand why you're leaving."

"The child needs looking after."

"That girl is no child if you hadn't noticed, and I suspect she can take care of herself well enough. You should be resting your bones."

"Plenty of time to rest when I'm dead, which may be sooner rather than later. Until then, I'd like to make myself useful."

Dorsit gave the tavern owner a kiss on the cheek and her color rose.

"You know, I've always been quite fond of you." She brushed a lock of his snowy white hair back from his drawn face. "I wish there was some way for you to regain your youth."

He averted his eyes. "What's done is done."

Her sigh was wistful. "I'll go pack you a bit of food to take with you on the road."

Before she could leave, Dorsit caught her wrist and poured several diamonds into her hand. "Thank you for everything. Maybe I'll be wanting my room back someday."

Her fingers closed around the stones. "You've got a place here, anytime."

For a few moments after she left, he allowed himself to wallow in self-pity at his weak, wasted body. He could do nothing to help his neighbors and very little to help Kira, but he would willingly draw his last breath trying to keep her safe.

Shortly thereafter, Dorsit set off for the fisherman's village, several hours' ride south of Ylan. The settlement was small, consisting only of a tavern and a few rude huts. Fishing boats were anchored in Ylan Bay, and the scent of fish permeated the cool clammy air. Alongside the pier, a small cargo vessel was moored so the fishermen could unload the day's catch. Dorsit hired the boat from a captain grateful for the extra work.

Twilight was gathering when Dorsit led his horse on board. After he made sure his mount was well-tended in the cargo hold, he returned to the deck to wait for Kira. Despite his frailty, he couldn't stop pacing from worry. From the crow's nest, one of the deckhands finally spied a horse and rider with the aid of a spyglass.

"She's coming," he called out.

Dorsit felt his shoulders relax ever so slightly. He hobbled to the railing and lifted his arms in a wave. Kira waved back, and a few minutes later she rode Myst down the pier. When she arrived, deckhands led the horse, lathered from exertion, onto the ship and into the cargo hold. Although Kira's face was etched with fatigue, Dorsit was relieved she seemed in good spirits. While she tended to her mount, he directed Captain Boon to weigh anchor as quickly as possible. As the ship set sail, Dorsit joined Kira in the cargo hold. He watched as she rubbed Myst down, checked her hooves for stones, and made sure the water and oat buckets were adequately filled.

"We are underway," he said. "I hope you don't get seasick."

"We'll see, won't we?"

Kira's boot brushed against a newtic in the straw, and its pop startled her. A curious expression of longing turned her eyes glassy.

"Are you unwell?" he asked.

A shutter descended. "I'm fine, thank you. I was just reminded of something."

Myst stuck her nose into the oat bucket and began to chew.

"Your horse has been taken care of," Dorsit said. "Let's go to the deck house and have something to eat. Then you can tell me about your escape."

~

A DINNER OF BREAD, cheese, fruit, and cold sliced chicken awaited Kira in the deck house. Famished, she made herself and Dorsit sandwiches while he got them something to drink.

"This is very good." She spoke through a mouthful of sandwich.

"Don't get too used to it." Dorsit chuckled. "I brought this food with me from the Two Moon Inn. I daresay breakfast on a fishing vessel won't be quite as edible, but we'll be at Gallina Point shortly thereafter."

When he set a mug of ale in front of her, Kira visibly recoiled. Ever since Mandral poisoned her, she hadn't viewed the beverage the same way.

"Is there any water?"

"Of course."

Although Dorsit said nothing, Kira could see him watching her as he removed the mug of ale and replaced it with one of water. Although she was trying to behave normally, fatigue was contributing to lapses of self-control. She'd overreacted just now to the ale, and in the cargo hold a few minutes ago, the newtics had reminded her of the stable where she'd hidden from Mandral. When she heard his voice, the poison had nearly caused her to run to the warlord and beg for his forgiveness.

"Don't look so guilty."

Her eyes widened. "What?"

"Many people don't like ale. I'm not offended in the least."

"Oh." Deep breath.

"Now tell me about your escape."

"Never before have I felt so much like a hunted animal. As I rode, I brushed Emberr's dress against trees and boulders. When I reached the cliff, I dismounted, scuffed around in the dirt, and then dropped the garment over the edge. I don't think it will fool the hounds for long, but maybe it will confuse the cygards."

"If Mandral knew who you were, why didn't he detain you in Eastknot?"

Because he believed me to be under his thrall. "H-He underestimated my ability to escape, I suppose."

Dorsit's blue eyes bored into hers until she cast about for another topic.

"Er...you promised to tell me how you could afford to hire this ship."

"Ah, yes."

He reached into the pocket of his robes, produced a leather pouch, and poured the contents on the table. A myriad of raw gemstones, predominately diamonds, lay before her.

"Efysian's cavern is littered with these. When I regained consciousness after being released from his spells, I realized rather quickly I was drained. Knowing I could no longer earn my living as a wizard, I took as many gemstones as I could fit into my pockets. The Guardian suggested it, actually."

"You spoke of her before. Who is she?"

"She never told me her name, but she's a powerful and immortal nymph tasked with guarding Efysian's lair. I'm not altogether certain her service to him is voluntary."

"What makes you think so?"

"Her slavish devotion to him is unnatural. I believe the Wolf Clan wizard has enthralled her somehow."

"How despicable." *I understand completely how she must feel.* Her face flamed with embarrassment and she stood. "It's a little warm in here. Do you suppose we could step outside for a little while?"

"Of course."

Yden's two moons cast twin paths of light on the undulating surface of Ylan Bay. Captain Pool was on deck, giving instructions to the nimble deckhands as to sails and rudders. Kira squinted her eyes, but she couldn't quite make out the shoreline in the inky darkness.

"I'm glad the captain knows how to navigate this ship in the dark," she said. "There are so many islands in the bay, I'm certain I would run her aground."

"I believe an old wizard friend of mine retired to one of these islands many turns ago. His name is Quixoran, and if I had my powers back I would transport us there. The shadow hounds couldn't track you under his protection."

Dorsit excused himself to see if their sleeping quarters were ready. While she waited, Kira breathed in fresh air and stared out at the black, glassy water. She should be at her father's side, using a sword to defend the territory, and instead she was fleeing from Mandral like a coward. Unbidden, the memory of the warlord's kisses flashed into her mind and her knees grew weak. *No, no, no!* She squeezed her eyes closed and tightened her desperate grip on the railing. *I hate him for doing this to me.*

Shaking from her inner struggle, Kira fervently wished Dorsit would hasten his return. Her fevered thoughts seemed to increase when she was alone, and she found the wizard's presence soothing. In a way, her pity for his diminished physical condition took her mind off her own incessant cravings. Although she didn't know how at that moment, she vowed to conquer her obsession. If not, she could very well envision a future of madness.

Dorsit's whisper light hand descended on her shoulder. "You're trembling."

"I-I'm cold," she lied.

"Come. Let me show you where you're to sleep tonight."

AN ARMOR-CLAD Rampen Szul peered at the blood-spattered scout who'd ridden all night long. As dawn broke, the conclave had assembled to hear his report.

"Squads of huge metal giants are marching toward Wyckcrest, as far as the eye can see," the scout said. "They'll be here within hours."

"How did you become injured?" Szul asked.

"This isn't my blood, sir. You told us not to engage the enemy, but one of the giants stepped out from the woods and took Lianyn's head off with a single blow of his ax. I believe the monsters anticipated us."

Szul dismissed the scout and bade the members of the conclave to ride east with him. He would not contemplate surrender until he'd seen this juggernaut for himself. There was little discussion as the Nomads mounted their chargers and rode through the forest until they reached the road. The Nomad leader was taken aback by the peculiar plume rising into the air from a distance.

"Is that smoke?" someone muttered.

Szul shook his head. "No. It's dust stirred by the approach of a mighty army."

He motioned his men to join him, two on either side. Five abreast, they urged their horses forward at a walk. For the next hour, birdcalls and the soft clop of horses' hooves were the only sounds to disturb the early morning calm. When the cygard army came within view, Szul's men blanched and reined in their horses, but the Nomad chief didn't pause or blink an eye.

A man with dark hair and painted eyes was leading the army, astride an impressive black charger. Although Szul guessed he was Warlord Mandral, he was taken aback by the man's relative youth and casual demeanor. Riding alongside was a wizard—Patnik, no doubt—identifiable by his rune etched robe and floppy wizard's cap. When Mandral and Szul were a mere twenty feet apart, both reined in their mounts.

"Mandral, I presume," Szul said.

His enemy's wicked smile caught the Nomad by surprise.

"In the flesh. And you must be Chief Rampen Szul."

Behind Szul, the Nomad conclave stirred when Mandral

dismounted. The Nomad leader held up his hand for calm. He dismounted and met Mandral and Patnik in the center of the road. The warlord gave him an appraising glance.

"You're quite tall. I can see where Kira gets her height."

Caught off guard by the innocuous comment, Szul stared. "What?"

"It's of little consequence. I suggest we go elsewhere to talk."

"You may accompany me back to my encampment at Wyck-crest, if you wish. I'll vouch for your safety personally."

Mandral's gaze flickered to Patnik. "I had something else in mind."

Before Szul could respond, the wizard touched his arm and Mandral's at the same time. A flash of light filled his vision and the sound of a rolling thunderclap reached his ears, and then the forest disappeared. To Szul's shock, the three men materialized inside an intimate dining room.

"Where are we?" he demanded.

"A private dining room at Eastknot Lodge," Mandral said. "I thought you could make yourself more comfortable here while we discuss the terms of your surrender."

SECRETS

Kira spent a miserable night on the ship, wrestling with her nightmarish dreams of Mandral. When dawn broke, however, she lay awake in her berth, worrying about her father and the fate of Nomad Territory. Her message of warning would have been far too late to overcome Mandral's element of surprise, and the warlord's Cyclopes army held an overwhelming advantage in terms of numbers and physical size. Like in Ylan, capitulation was the only logical choice—but the idea rankled. Until her father could determine how to oust the warlord, Nomad Territory was very likely lost.

If only she'd known earlier what Mandral's intentions were, she would have cut his throat at Eastknot. Even at this late date, an assassination would put his forces in disarray, but who could get close enough to execute him? If the warlord were out in the open, a crack archer like Reye could dispatch him, but if some unseen magic protected the warlord, retribution would be harsh and brutal. No sooner had she envisioned Mandral lying on the ground with an arrow through his throat than a surge of emotion made her sob with grief. She would rather die than see any harm come to him.

Nonsense! Such thoughts were the residual effects of the poison, and she could no longer allow her emotions to dictate her behavior. Whatever her imagined feelings were for the warlord, she still had her logic and intelligence intact. If she had the opportunity to kill Mandral, she would take it—no matter how much she suffered. Kira blotted her tears and left her tiny cabin to walk in the bracing morning air. The sky overhead was overcast, to her dismay. A full day's journey lay ahead, and a rainstorm would only add to the misery.

The fishing vessel docked at Gallina Point mid-morning. Kira and Dorsit disembarked and led their horses from the pier up a winding road paved with cobblestones. They stopped for food at a tavern near the main thoroughfare, grateful for some hot food after their chilly night on the water. After he'd assuaged his hunger, Dorsit sat back and watched Kira finish her breakfast.

"We outwitted the cygards and outfoxed the shadow hounds. Where are we heading next?" he asked.

"I can go no longer without knowing if the Territory has fallen. If we take Tradewynd Road north, Wyckcrest is three days from here. I want to go home."

MANDRAL GAVE SZUL A CHARMING SMILE. "You needn't think of this as a conquest. Once I've married your daughter, I'll be your legitimate heir."

Szul was bewildered. "My eldest daughter has recently married Warlord Laramy and is out of your grasp."

"I refer to Kira, of course," Mandral said. "She gave me her word as a Nomad that she would become my bride."

Szul stared across the table, convinced the warlord was out of his mind. "That's impossible! It was she who alerted me to your invasion!"

"And I applaud her for it. Having seen the superiority of my forces, undoubtedly she wished you to realize the futility of resistance before casualties could mount."

"This is absurd! Kira has only fifteen turns, sir. Here in Nomad Territory, females don't marry until they've reached the age of sixteen at least."

"A few more months makes no difference. A betrothal will suit my purposes, and our impending wedding will be anticipated by one and all."

Mandral snapped his finger at a thin bald man in the back of the room, who was making notes on a scroll of parchment. "You there...what's your name?"

"Tyrg."

"Draw up a contract between myself and Kira Szul and include the stipulation she must present herself to me on her sixteenth birthday."

The warlord turned back to Szul. "She won't have far to travel. You and I shall be neighbors, you know. I intend to build a castle near Wyckcrest."

Mandral's confident smile infuriated Szul. Had the warlord's men not already relieved him of his sword, he would have drawn the blade.

"I refuse to accept that my daughter has agreed to marry you."

"You wound me, sir. She and I were captivated with one another from the moment we met."

"Until I hear that from her lips, I won't believe it."

"Perhaps you'll believe it from another trusted source."

At Mandral's nod, the doors to the room opened and Reye was brought in. His handsome face was battered and his clothes were torn, but he managed to walk without assistance. Mandral bade him take a seat at the table, and had the attendants pour him a goblet of water. Reye sucked the liquid down greedily, and it seemed clear to Szul the man had been through an ordeal.

"I apologize for Reye's condition, but my cygards don't really understand the concept of handling someone gently," Mandral said. "Reye has personal knowledge of Kira's affections. I'll give you a few minutes of privacy to discuss the matter."

True to his word, the warlord left the room, taking his men with him. As soon as the door shut, Reye began to apologize for not protecting Kira better.

"Enough of that for now," Szul said. "Mandral claims Kira agreed to marry him. Could there be any truth to this?"

Reye's eyebrows rose. "I suppose it's possible. She seemed quite taken with him when the three of us dined together. They shared an interest in alchemy and such, but I never heard him make an offer for her hand."

"Perhaps they met alone?"

The young warrior blanched visibly. "After dinner, Mandral escorted Kira to her room, but he returned no more than ten minutes later."

Szul clenched his fist. "He's a handsome man, admittedly, but Kira is not the sort of girl to give over her affections on a whim."

"No, nor have her actions been otherwise out of character. She saved my life from Mandral's assassin the next morning. She'd learned of the invasion somehow and was determined to seek Dorsit's help in Ylan. I was caught, but she escaped."

"Those were not the actions of a woman in love." Szul pinched the bridge of his nose, perplexed.

"I must admit, however, Kira acted besotted with Mandral, and he with her—even though she didn't know about the invasion yet," Reye said. "She changed her opinion when she realized what he was about."

"Be that as it may, Nomads don't make promises they can't keep. If she promised to marry him, her word is binding."

A quick knock at the door announced Mandral's return. The

warlord glanced from Szul to Reye and back again, with an attitude of expectation. "So are we agreed?"

"Draw up the contract," Szul said. "But unless my daughter signs it in person, I will not hold her to it."

The warlord rubbed his hands together. "I wouldn't have it otherwise. Now, in the meantime I'll order my cygards to practice forbearance. As long as our truce holds, no one must suffer."

Mandral's definition of truce was indistinguishable from an outright occupation, just as a cygard's notion of forbearance was likely akin to his ability to be gentle. Nevertheless, Szul nodded his assent. Having seen the enemy, he had no other choice.

KIRA BIT her lip as she watched Dorsit's frustrated efforts to conjure another courier bird. An entire day had passed since disembarking at Gallina Point, but the wizard hadn't managed to work any magic whatsoever. They'd stopped at Tradewynd River to water the horses and to rest a short while, but Dorsit wouldn't be satisfied until he'd tried the spell yet again.

"I'm so sorry," he said finally. "It's possible my magic is completely gone now."

His wretched expression tore at her heart. "Never mind. Come, let's sit in the shade for a while."

They settled themselves underneath a pillow tree, which possessed a trunk flexible enough to provide a comfortable backrest.

"At least we don't have to contend with rain today," he said. "Yesterday was rather miserable."

"You didn't complain once. I'm continually amazed at how you look on the bright side of life."

"It does no good to brood."

"I find myself doing just that all too frequently." She gave him a smile. "There is a tavern at Mirror Pond not too far from here, where we can get a midday meal. Perhaps once you've eaten, you'll feel more magical."

"Yes, I'll try again after I eat. Like you, I'm anxious for news."

Kira rested the back of her head against the pliable bark of the pillow tree and watched the wide river flow past. The warm temperature combined with yet another sleepless night and she found herself drifting off into a wonderful dream. Mandral was kissing her with increasing passion, but in the next moment, Gant and Aion arrived out of nowhere to haul him away. As she screamed Mandral's name, Reye appeared, taking aim with his bow and arrow. She ran to shield Mandral just as the arrow flew. The sharp missile pierced her chest instead, and she awoke with a start. To her dismay, her head was cradled in Dorsit's lap and he was stroking her hair with his bony hand.

"I must have fallen asleep." Embarrassed, she sat up, passing a trembling hand over her face. "I hope I didn't drool on you."

He didn't smile at her joke, and she could see pity in his eyes.

"How did it happen?" he asked.

"What do you mean?"

"Mandral gave you a love potion."

A gasp. "Did Adrea tell you that?"

"No, but I've suspected it for some time. You talked in your sleep at the Two Moon Inn." He paused. "I didn't want to believe it at first, but the symptoms are unmistakable."

"Symptoms?"

"The poison manifests itself in tremors, nightmares, flushed skin, and a feverish look to the eyes, accompanied by obsessive thoughts and irrational behavior. You've kept your behavior under control, and that's what I can't understand. How do you manage?"

A crushing wave of shame swept over her, followed by a sense of relief she didn't have to hide her condition from Dorsit any longer.

"When I realized he'd poisoned me, I took an emetic—too late to do much good, I'm afraid."

"I applaud your quick thinking. If you hadn't taken the emetic, you wouldn't have had the ability to escape or warn your father. You'd never have another independent thought again, in fact. I've seen the effects of a love potion before, and things didn't end well for the man who was poisoned."

Kira dropped her face in her hands. "I'm so ashamed. You must promise not to tell anyone, ever."

"I won't, but there's nothing to be ashamed of."

"If people knew I was obsessed by that monster, they'd never look at me the same way. I must keep it a secret."

"You have a point. Your allegiance would always be in question, even if we found a cure."

"There's no cure, according to Adrea."

"You told her your troubles?"

"No, I merely asked about love potions in general. She said the only thing to keep the poison at bay would be to avoid contact with the poisoner altogether. That's why I couldn't allow myself to be captured. If I'm near Mandral, I'm afraid I won't be able to control myself."

"Having watched you fight the poison these last few days, I'm certain you can. Be assured, I won't give up looking for an antidote."

A crooked grin found its way to her lips. "We're quite a pair, aren't we? I want to find a cure for you, and you want to find an antidote for me."

His eyes crinkled at the edges. "You're worse off than I am. I may look old, but at least I have peace of mind."

She helped Dorsit to his feet and gave him a hug. "Thank you. Only you could make me laugh at myself."

"My pleasure. Let's ride on to Mirror Pond. I'm quite eager to see if a good meal will reenergize my magic."

Even after she and Dorsit ate lunch, however, he was still

unable to conjure the courier bird. They continued their trek northward, pausing only to ask travelers passing by if they'd come from Wyckcrest. Having shared her horrible secret with Dorsit, Kira's heart felt a little lighter. The relief was outweighed, however, by an ever-increasing certainty the Nomad encampment would be soaked in blood when she arrived.

In the late afternoon, they encountered a farmer heading south with a largely empty wagon. Kira flagged him down. "Have you by any chance come from Wyckcrest?"

The man nodded. "I managed to sell all my corn yesterday and got a bargain on some blankets to boot."

"Is there any news from Wyckcrest?" she asked. "Anything out of the ordinary?"

The farmer scratched his head. "Well…traffic was lighter than usual, and half the booths were closed. I heard there was a downed tree blocking the road to the east."

Kira and Dorsit thanked the man and wished him safe travel. As she and Dorsit rode on, they sorted through the possibilities.

"Mandral's army could be massed outside Wyckcrest, waiting for something," he said.

"Yes. If Mandral had accomplished a complete coup, he would have ridden into Wyckcrest by now, with his flags blazing. And if the Nomads had put up resistance, word of casualties would certainly have reached Wyckcrest Village."

"This is all very strange."

She sighed. "I suppose we'll know more when we reach the encampment tomorrow."

"Indeed we will."

As Kira squared her shoulders and lifted her chin, Dorsit's admiration for her bravery increased. Although crippled by

Mandral's poison, she was determined to face the future like a Nomad. If he had some of his strength back, maybe he could be more help. Inwardly, he cursed Efysian for taking his magic away. Despite Dorsit's assertions to the contrary, he actually brooded a great deal about his condition. But like Kira, he'd tried not to let his emotions control his behavior.

As he glanced at her, another feeling took root in his heart, one he thought himself too old to ever feel again. Perhaps not too old, he corrected himself. Too drained. He might look ancient, but he was only twenty-four. Before he was kidnapped, he'd regarded Kira as merely Kysandra's little sister, in braids and boys' clothing. Since then, she'd blossomed into an extraordinary young woman whose face and figure had ripened beyond her turns. Her violet eyes could soften even the hardest hearts, and her glorious chestnut hair drifted about her shoulders and down her back like a magical cloak. He had no doubt in a turn or two she would achieve the sort of physical beauty that men would fight and perhaps even die for. *Oh, I'm a pitiful, romantic fool.* He tried to push his wistful feelings away. *She could never look at me now.*

BE IT RESOLVED

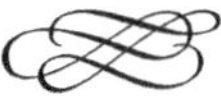

A squad of Nomad warriors intercepted Kira and Dorsit as they approached the Nomad encampment the following day. Having never seen Kira with her hair loose, they challenged her as a stranger. When she drew her blade with an offer to prove her identity as Rampen Szul's daughter, the warriors exchanged startled glances with one another.

"Forgive us, Princess. We didn't recognize you."

She sheathed her sword. "How goes the conflict with Warlord Mandral?"

"There is a truce…for now. We'll escort you to camp."

Dorsit apparently recognized one of the men. "Arti? It's Dorsit of the Leopard Clan."

The warrior curled his lip. "That's absurd, old man, and my friend wouldn't thank you for trying to steal his name."

The drawn skin over Dorsit's cheekbones grew flushed. "I've been drained, Arti, but it's me. I can no longer drink you under the table, but I daresay I could still best you in cards."

Arti stared in disbelief, as did the other warriors.

"Dorsit is who he says he is." The edge in her voice was deliberate. "You'd do well to make him feel at home."

Without waiting for a response, she urged her mare into a gallop. Sensing the journey was at its end, Myst needed little encouragement.

"Wait!" Arti called out, but she paid him no heed.

When the pavilion tent came into view, several cygards blocked Kira's path. Myst reared up on her hind legs in a panic, and Kira was thrown to the ground. The cygards raised their axes, but the Nomad squad arrived just then with their swords drawn. Arti jumped from his horse and shielded her with his body.

"Stop! This is Rampen Szul's daughter, newly arrived. She didn't realize an escort was required!"

The cygards burst into mocking laughter. "You should school the female before she gets hurt."

"And you should step back and give the Princess some air."

As Kira struggled to breathe, she wondered if she'd heard correctly. *An escort is required in my own encampment?* Arti helped her to stand, grabbing her wrist when she reached for her sword.

"*Don't,*" he murmured. "Cygards are all over this camp, spoiling to cover their ax blades with our blood."

Kira relaxed her sword arm. "Take me to my father."

She gathered up Myst's reins and led her past the metal giants, giving each of them the ugliest glare possible. Arti led his own mount alongside. Scanning her surroundings more carefully, she now spied cygards everywhere, leaning up against trees or guarding tents.

"This is no truce," she whispered. "Has anyone been killed?"

"Only one we know for sure. A scout—Lianyn."

Kira closed her eyes as horror washed over her. "Lianyn was a good man."

"There may be others, but we've been prevented by cygards from leaving the immediate vicinity to check."

Her mouth grew dry as she formed her next question. "Has there been any word from Reye?"

"He's battered, but he'll live. The wizard transported him back with your father."

Sweet relief was followed closely by confusion. "Transported back with my father from where? I don't understand."

"Much has happened since your father heard from you last. Direct your questions to him."

Arti's tone was decidedly cool, as if he laid blame at her feet. Although she flicked a puzzled glance in his direction, the Nomad ignored her. She'd left Eastknot to get help and sent a warning to her father as soon as possible. What more could she have done?

SEVERAL CYGARDS WERE PACING outside her father's tent when Kira arrived. She handed off Myst's reins to Arti and asked him to take the mare to the stables.

"And can you find some suitable quarters for Dorsit, please? He'll be staying with us."

More fearlessly than she felt, Kira pushed past the cygards and entered the tent. Her father rushed over to envelop her in his warm embrace.

"I've been so worried about you. Why didn't Dorsit send another courier bird?"

"He's been unable to work any magic at all for days," she said. "And you must prepare yourself, Father. He resembles a very old man now."

His expression was bleak. "Can nothing be done?"

"He thinks not, but I'm determined to prove him wrong."

A flash of light and a thunderclap outside heralded the arrival of Patnik—but the wizard was not alone. Mandral stepped inside the tent with a gleam in his obsidian eyes. Kira's gasp of horror transformed itself into a sigh, and although her feet remained rooted to the spot, she yearned to rush into his arms. She felt blood rushing to her cheeks, and an intoxicating sensation made her suddenly giddy. *Poison.*

"Mandral." His name felt like a caress.

"I heard you were back."

When the warlord slipped his arms around her waist and pressed his lips against hers, his touch was her undoing. After they kissed, he moved his lips to her ear.

"You were very naughty to run away. I'm disappointed."

His hot breath sent intoxicating sensations down her spine. Her arms tightened around him. "I'm so sorry. It was wrong."

"If you disappoint me again, I'll have to punish someone. Reye, perhaps, or your father?"

"No!" She nestled into his chest, reveling in his fragrance. "Give me another chance."

"You're going to have to prove your devotion."

"Anything. I'll do anything you wish."

Her father cleared his throat. Although Mandral released Kira, he kept her hand tightly clasped in his. So engrossed was she in memorizing the beautiful planes of Mandral's countenance, she barely heard her father speak.

"I see my daughter's affections for you are indisputable, Warlord. All that remains is for her to sign the contract."

Mandral led her to the table, dipped the pen in a well of ink, and slipped it into her hand. The act seemed such an intimate one, she began to tremble with euphoria.

"Sign here, my love, and we will be betrothed," he said.

Bending over the parchment, Kira scratched her name where Mandral told her she should. Afterward, she felt such delight in pleasing him that tears sprang to her eyes.

"You've made me very happy," she said.

He kissed her on the forehead before rolling up the parchment and handing it off to Patnik, who stood nearby with a carefully neutral expression.

"I have much to do, so I'll take my leave," Mandral said.

Her heart plummeted and she caught his arm. "Must you go so soon?"

"Your sixteenth birthday will also be our wedding day. In the meantime, I have a territory to establish."

Mandral deposited a final kiss on her cheek. After he left with Patnik, she dropped into a chair, suddenly calm. The sensations she'd felt at Mandral's presence had been authentic, but in an effort to feign complete subjugation, she'd made no attempt to control them. Since Mandral had effectively taken over the territory, nothing else could be done at the moment except submit—for now. *His poison may run through my veins, but he'll pay for what he's done. On my sixteenth birthday he'll expect a simpering, breathless bride...but he'll receive a bloodthirsty assassin instead.*

Her father knelt before her and took her hand. "Are you sure about this?"

As Kira searched his face, she saw a noble man, bent but not broken. "Even if I weren't, we have no choice."

THE LEOPARD CLAN wizard was playing cards with Aion, Arti, and Gant, when Lane and Hyrn entered the tent. As Lane dragged a chair over to the table, he said something which made Dorsit consider whether he was losing his hearing along with his wits.

"Kira did *what?*"

"She signed a contract of engagement with Warlord Mandral," Lane repeated. "The announcements are posted all over town."

"I'd heard rumors she'd promised to marry him," Arti said. "I was hoping they were lies."

"I'm going to be sick." Gant pulled a face. "How *could* she?"

"She's a bloody traitor," Aion muttered. "I wouldn't have thought she'd sink that low."

"You don't know what you're talking about." Dorsit's tone was sharp. "If Kira agreed to marry him, it was to save Nomad lives. Cygards were as thick as the trees when I rode into the encampment earlier today, if you hadn't noticed. Now, most of them have withdrawn."

"I'd rather *die* than see Nomad blood mixed with that Warlord Mongrel," Hyrn said.

"Mandral," Arti said.

"No, I said Mongrel and I meant it," Hyrn said. "And I consider Rampen Szul a coward for not choosing to fight."

A short, stunned silence ensued. Insults flew as Nomads bickered and chose sides. Dorsit held up his withered hands for calm.

"Lads, lay your anger at the feet of the invaders, not your leaders. Put away your hostilities and let me deal the cards. And if I hear one more negative word about Kira, I won't be responsible for what follows."

Although that last part was a bluff, Dorsit counted on the warriors not knowing exactly how much he'd been drained. After a few awkward moments, however, tempers cooled and the Nomads warily returned to their game. Dorsit shuffled the deck and began to deal the cards, but in the back of his mind he couldn't put the vision of Mandral and Kira out of his mind. She'd achieved an admirable level of control where the warlord was concerned, so why would she agree to such a union now? *Unless the engagement isn't exactly what it seems.*

~

DISCONSOLATE, Kira stood in a clearing and unleashed yet another barrage of knives at the semi-circle of targets. When she retrieved the knives, she turned to discover Reye waiting for her. The bruises on his face had disappeared and she noted the angry red cut on his jawline was nearly healed.

"You look almost normal," she said.

"My shoulder is still sore, but I'll be back to seducing young women shortly."

"I'll spread the word." Her brief laugh faded all too quickly. "You shouldn't be here. If anyone sees you talking to me, you'll be an unwelcome drinking partner." Her jest held more than a kernel of truth.

His expression grew cloudy. "I've told the warriors they're being unfair, you know. If it wasn't for your betrothal, we'd all be dead by now."

"Yes, but I'm fraternizing with the enemy." She kicked at a pinecone. "Most Nomads would have rather fought than submit, and some would rather see me dead than Mandral's intended."

He winced but did not refute her statement. "I came to say good-bye, actually. Mandral's people have issued me a travel pass. I'm riding to Eastknot to retrieve Ladies' Man. He was left behind when Patnik transported your father and me back here."

Although she felt bereft at the news of her friend's imminent departure, she forced a smile to her face. Apart from Dorsit and her father, Reye was the only one in the camp who would speak to her.

"Have a safe journey."

"Thank you." He paused. "The warlord has issued some new edicts, by the way."

"More edicts? He would do better to forbid everything and get it over with."

Reye was taken aback. "A curious attitude toward your future bridegroom."

In a flash of anger, Kira hurled a knife at the target furthest away. The knife buried itself to the hilt, dead center. "My feelings toward Mandral are…complicated." *But things will become far simpler at the point of my knife.* "What sorts of edicts must we cope with now?"

Reye produced a parchment from his pocket and skimmed the contents. "Wyckcrest is called Mandral Village now."

A sound of disgust issued from Kira's throat.

"Every citizen is to surrender his or her gold and silver in exchange for a new form of currency called tile," Reye continued. "And head coverings must be worn in public, according to one's profession."

She gave him a crooked smile and lowered her voice. "I wonder what sort of head covering signifies 'rebel'?"

He glanced around to make sure they weren't overheard. "So you really *aren't* giving up?"

"Not until my final breath, Reye. And not even then."

The two warriors embraced each other, as if for the last time.

Kira cleared out her sister's remaining belongings from her tent. Thrilled to have the space to herself, she created her own sitting area and workbench, where she prepared everything from fragrances to tea. She was particularly keen to start Dorsit on a regular regimen of the grail mushroom tea Adrea had recommended. The mushrooms were abundant in the fields nearby, so she gathered a basketful, sliced and dried them, and then boiled a quantity of ground mushroom for the tea. Dorsit came to her tent every afternoon for a cup, although he wasn't particularly fond of the taste.

When Dorsit arrived for his tea one afternoon, Kira began to see an improvement. The wizard seemed to stand a bit straighter, and his face was not nearly so drawn. In addition, his disposition had taken on a slight edge of rebellion. He sat at the table, took a whiff of freshly brewed tea, and grimaced.

"You're sure this is restorative?"

Kira compressed her lips together to avoid laughing and pushed a bowl of sugar in his direction. "Come on, it smells worse than it tastes." As if to prove her point, she sipped from her own cup.

The wizard stirred a heaping teaspoonful of sugar into the steaming fluid, raised the cup to his lips, and drank. A shudder ensued.

"Don't be a baby. Admit it, the tea has given you back a bit of energy."

"I have no trouble admitting it, I just don't enjoy drinking the tea."

"Oftentimes it's necessary to do unpleasant things." She averted her eyes. "As I know, full well."

"Is that why you agreed to marry Mandral?"

"Somebody has to get close enough to kill him."

"Will you be able carry out the act even though your feelings forbid it?"

"You're able to drink that tea, even though you don't like it."

"Drinking tea isn't the same thing."

"Perhaps this tea will fortify my resolve." Kira drained her cup.

"I've been thinking; the Mirrum Mountain nymphs are versed in herbology and may hold the solution to my renewal and your antidote."

A scowl. "I'd never ask anything from a nymph."

"I've no such scruples. If you don't wish to accompany me, I'll go alone."

"The Mirrum Mountains are in the southwest quadrant of Nomad Territory. That's a long and difficult journey, Dorsit. Can you transport there?"

"I'm afraid transporting is still beyond me, but unless I get more strength than is available from this grail mushroom tea, my magic may fade entirely."

Kira's heart felt as if someone were squeezing it.

"I won't let that happen. Unfortunately, travel will prove problematic since Mandral will undoubtedly deny our applications for travel passes." She paused. "We'd have to obtain forgeries."

"I know someone in the village who's handy with such things."

Her lips curved into a smile. "How soon can we leave?"

AT WHAT PRICE

Not far from the village, Mandral's castle was under construction over the ruins of an ancient fortress. With the help of Patnik's magic and Cyclopes laborers, a large part of the structure was completed in a short period of time. During the day, the warlord conducted business within view of the rising edifice, underneath a canopy to shield him from the suns. Months had passed since he'd seized Nomad Territory, and his lack of a throne room and all the accoutrements of victory had begun to chafe. He sent someone to fetch Patnik. The wizard transported nearby in a flash of light and thunder.

"You wished to see me, Warlord?"

"I grow impatient living out of a tent like a Nomad. When will the castle be completed?"

"I believe it may be eight weeks yet."

"You have a fortnight."

"I don't know if it can be done!"

"Don't fail me, wizard. You wouldn't like the consequences."

Patnik's eyes widened in panic. "The living quarters in one wing are nearly finished now."

"Prepare rooms for me, and an adjoining room for my bride-to-be. I intend to sleep there tonight."

In a dither, the wizard disappeared. Not long thereafter, the commander of his cygard army approached, helmet in hand. As Captain Blane spoke, Mandral's gaze wandered to the construction in the background. He had no wish to stare at the oozing sores that marked the Cyclop's face.

"I sent several cygards to round up the nymphs at the river, Warlord," Blane said. "Unfortunately, the cygards were found just now, drowned."

"The nymphs' loyalty to the Nomads must not go unchallenged. Disarm the Nomads. Destroy their weapons and kill anyone who fights back. I'm the ruler of this territory, no one else."

"Shall we kill Rampen Szul?"

"No. I don't want him to become a martyr—yet. Escort Kira here. She's to reside with me in the castle from now on."

As Blane turned away, his face split in a leering grin. The sound of a wizard's transport curled Mandral's lip.

"Why have you returned, Patnik? It will be your head if—" the warlord broke off when he realized the newcomer was a different wizard entirely. "Who are you?"

Dark-haired and sleek, the man sketched a bow "Efysian of the Wolf Clan, at your service."

Taken aback, Mandral frowned. "You can't be the Wolf Clan wizard. He's an extremely old man."

Efysian's yellow eyes glittered as he held up his clan ring. "I can assure you, I am he. I understand you've established yourself as the warlord in this Territory. I came to offer you an alliance."

"I have a wizard already."

"The Turtle Clan wizard?" Efysian scoffed. "He will fail you."

"So far he has done what I ask."

The wizard tossed Mandral a small drawstring bag. "Inside

that purse is a gold coin with the imprint of a wolf. If you have need of my services in the future, you need only turn it over in your hand three times and I will come."

The abrupt flash of light from Efysian's transport caused the warlord to blink. When his vision cleared, the wizard was gone.

"My dislike of wizards increases with every passing moment."

Nevertheless, the warlord slipped the purse into his pocket.

WHILE DORSIT WENT off to obtain the forged travel documents, she packed a knapsack for the long journey ahead. Her dour mood had lifted at the thought of a quest. Even if the Mirrum Mountain nymphs were unable to help, they might know someone who could. A commotion outside drew her from her tent. When she emerged, she discovered a tsunami of cygards had descended on the encampment. The armor-clad Cyclopes were striding into tents unannounced and emerging with swords and other weapons. The Nomads' angry protests were ignored, and the cygards tossed the weapons into a wagon near the pavilion. *Mandral is disarming us!*

Kira darted toward her father's tent, to warn him. As she approached, she saw her father struggling to prevent two cygards from confiscating his ancient ceremonial sword. Without considering the prudence of her actions, she launched herself at the one closest to her, aiming a flying sidekick at the back of his knee. The cygard's leg buckled on impact, and he stumbled forward. With a downward ax kick, she knocked him to the ground. Her father used the distraction to wrest himself away from the second cygard, at which point Kira drew her sword and separated the cygard's head from his shoulders. To her dismay, her blade shattered on his armor. Surrounded by infuriated cygards, she had no weapon to defend herself. Her father brandished his sword at the approaching giants.

"*Run*, Kira," he commanded. "They've come to take you as well."

She dropped the useless haft of her sword and sped toward the stables. Nomads closed ranks as they tried to aid her escape, but the armored giants tossed the unarmed men aside like toys. When she was fully surrounded, she had no choice but to surrender.

The captain of the cygards strode forward. "I'm to escort you to the warlord, Kira Szul. You're to reside at the castle from now on."

Despite the sweat on her brow from the fight, Kira shivered at the implications. As the warlord's face flashed into her mind, she squeezed her eyes shut and bit the inside of her cheek until she tasted blood.

"This is not in our agreement!" Szul roared. "My daughter remains with me until the wedding!"

Six cygards approached him with axes raised over their heads.

"Stop!" Kira screamed. "I'll go. Leave him alone and I'll go quietly."

The axes lowered more slowly than she would have wished, but at least the painful grip on her upper arms eased. She slid a look toward her father and gave him a nod.

"No matter where I wander, as a Nomad I will keep my promises." Her words were as deliberate as possible.

A brief flash of confusion on Szul's face was replaced by understanding. "Be safe."

She glanced up at the cygards flanking her. "Follow me to my tent. I must change into something more pleasing to the warlord."

The armor-clad guards clanked along behind as she took the shortest route to her tent. All around her, cygards resumed collecting swords and weapons. None of the Nomads would look her in the eye, and her throat began to ache. *They despise me and always will as long as Mandral controls the territory.* She ducked into her tent with a mumbled, "Wait here."

Out of the cygards' view, she shrugged on her knife-lined jacket and stuffed her traveling cloak inside her knapsack. As carefully and quietly as possible, she slit the fabric of her tent along a seam with a hunting knife and stepped outside—straight into the arms of a waiting cygard. Although she managed to plunge her blade through his eye visor, his scream alerted every cygard in the vicinity. Her adrenaline surged and she fled, ducking in between the narrow opening between two tents and then into a densely wooded area. Cygards were everywhere, and she wondered how long she could evade them. A glance over her shoulder revealed a squad of the one-eyed giants crashing through the trees in her direction. *If this goes on much longer, they'll pursue me until I drop from exhaustion.*

Counting on the cygards' heavy armor to slow them down, she ran uphill. When she could see them no longer, she turned sharply south. As she approached the hot spring pool, the three half-naked nymphs with skin the color of aquamarine and sapphire materialized and motioned her over. Although she recognized Elle, Glory, and Delphine, she'd never before exchanged more than a few words with them.

"Hide behind that rock," Elle whispered.

Unsure why she trusted her well-being to nymphs, Kira dove behind the stone shelf where the warm water bubbled up. Over a dozen cygards poured from the woods, and she gripped her knapsack to keep from bolting in fear.

"Where'd she go?" a booming voice demanded.

The trio of nymphs giggled.

"She dove into the water, but what's your hurry, One-Eye?" Elle replied.

The giant growled a sound of disgust, and then Kira heard the clanking of armor as the cygards clustered around the pool.

"Don't see her," the cygard grunted.

Glory giggled. "She's at the bottom, you big silly."

"Look closer," Delphine urged.

A few moments later, the sound of churning water was followed by choked screams and frantic splashing which gradually grew calm. In the ensuing silence, Kira heard Delphine calling her name. "You can come out now."

Pushing herself up with her arms, Kira peeked over the top of the rock. The cygards had fallen into the pool and sunk to the bottom, where they remained. She gasped in shock.

"What happened?"

"They wanted a closer look at the bottom of the pool so we gave it to them," Elle said.

The nymphs' tinkling laughter resembled rainfall, and Kira felt a tinge of remorse for all the critical things she'd ever thought about them.

"Thank you for helping me."

"Actually, we did it for revenge," Elle said.

Delphine pouted. "Cygards surrounded us at the river this morning and tried to catch us in nets."

"We drowned them instead," Glory said.

Kira peered at the nymphs, taken aback. She hadn't realized nymphs could be so powerful. *Perhaps the Mirrum Mountain nymphs can help Dorsit after all.* Although she longed to find the wizard and continue their quest together as they'd planned, Mandral's actions had made that impossible. She'd make the journey alone and bring the cure back to Dorsit. By then, her sixteenth birthday would be nigh.

～

AFTER EVERY WEAPON was stripped from the Nomad encampment and hauled away, Rampen Szul called his conclave together for an emergency meeting under the pavilion. As he began to speak, the water nymph Elle appeared and settled herself on a bench to listen.

"The warlord will not take the death of two cygards lightly, nor will he forgive Kira's escape," Szul said.

"It wasn't only two cygards who died," Elle said. "My sisters and I drowned several in the river this morning and a dozen more in the hot spring when they tried to capture Kira."

Szul blanched. "Did she get away?"

"Yes, but take warning. No witnesses remain to say the cygards died at the hands of nymphs and not Nomads. Delphine, Glory, and I are leaving, and that's what I came to tell you."

"We must pack up our tents and leave as well," Szul said.

One of the chieftains raised a question. "Where will we go?"

A muscle worked in the chief's jaw. "To ensure our very survival, I believe the Nomads should break into tribes and scatter. There are refuge caves in the foothills to the north as well as a large swath of thick woods in the center of the territory. We can survive there."

A collective moan of disbelief spread across the gathering.

"All this because Kira balked at the agreement she made? I say we track her down and deliver her to Mandral ourselves," someone shouted.

With no swords available, a fistfight broke out between the speaker and the surrounding Nomads. Szul raised his hands for calm and the skirmish died down.

"My daughter agreed to marry the warlord because she knew it would forestall greater harm to the people she loved. Your comment dishonors her sacrifice."

He allowed his statement to sink in before he continued speaking.

"She's still bound to fulfill her contract of engagement on her sixteenth birthday, but Mandral was not within his rights to require her presence at the castle now. Had she complied, it wouldn't have prevented our disarmament. We must disperse and rearm ourselves if we are ever to have a chance at winning back the territory."

THROUGH THE LIBERAL use of Patnik's magic, Mandral's living quarters had been completed and furnished with the finest carpets, wall hangings, draperies and a magnificent canopy over the wide bed. In his sitting room, a sizable desk and impressively carved chair awaited his use, along with luxurious chaise lounges and upholstered tuffets. None of the magnificence seemed to register with the warlord, however, as he raged at Captain Blane. Blane's second-in-command stood near the doorway, at attention. Patnik perched on a tuffet, his skin pale.

"What do you mean Kira *slipped away?*" Mandral demanded.

The captain tightened his grip on the helmet in his hands. "Although she pretended to cooperate at first, she escaped. Two cygards were killed in the process and a dozen more were drowned when they tried to track her."

Mandral's hearty laugh rang out. "A young girl of fifteen managed to best that many?"

Blane exchanged an uneasy glance with the cygard at the door. In the next moment, a sharp knife flew from the warlord's fingers, sailed through the air, and embedded itself in Blane's skull. The captain crashed to the ground in a heap of metal, and the warlord snapped his fingers at the remaining cygard soldier. "What's your name?"

"Isore, Warlord."

"You're now Captain. Have the Nomads been successfully disarmed?"

The newly elevated cygard blinked. "Yes, Warlord."

"Good. Burn the encampment." Mandral gestured toward Blane. "And get this mess out of here."

"It will be done." The captain stepped out of the room.

Mandral paced out of frustration. "Kira Szul should have been eager to heed my summons. This is the second time she has escaped me, and she must be brought to heel. I mean to wed and bed her—not necessarily in that order—before she's executed. What can be done to retrieve the girl?"

"I can conjure more shadow hounds."

"Perhaps, but I'd also like to know what Kira's up to. Do you have any other ideas?"

Patnik scratched his head. "Yes…but it's extraordinarily difficult and there are risks."

"I don't care. Do it."

CLAD IN A HOODED, full-length green traveling cloak, Kira hiked southbound through the woods, keeping Tradewynd River on her right. With each mile, the emptiness in her stomach continued to grow until she could think of nothing else. Although every Nomad could hunt for food, she was ill-prepared to do so; the rope she needed for snares was coiled in her saddlebag back in the stables and she'd had to sacrifice her hunting knife during the escape. The three-inch throwing knives lining her vest would be useful if she came across a rabbit, but she'd seen none that day. Wild berries and pine nuts sustained her somewhat, but when the suns began their downward trek, she decided she would have to eat a hot meal.

As she paused to drink some water from the river, she noticed Addertown on the far side. Unfortunately, the nearest bridge was patrolled by cygards who appeared to be harassing anyone attempting to cross. About a mile downstream, however, she knew of a fishing spot where the river was wider and calmer. Perhaps one of the fishermen could be bribed to ferry her to the other side, no questions asked.

When she arrived, a huge man with burly arms was sitting in a rowboat at the side of the river, as if waiting for someone.

"How are the fish?" she asked.

"Jumping from the nets. Seems they don't have proper travel permits."

"I understand their dilemma. What price?" she asked.

"A silver coin, if you please."

"Not tile?"

"Bah! Silver or nothing."

Fortunately, she'd packed gold and silver coins in her knapsack, in addition to tile. After paying for her passage, she settled herself in the rowboat, and the man rowed her to the far side. With the hood of her travel cloak pulled low, Kira headed into Addertown and stopped at the first reputable tavern she encountered. A little daylight still seeped in through the windows and lamps sat on every table, but she sat in a darkened corner and turned the wick on her lamp down low for privacy. The food set before her was humble, but she ate every last scrap and ordered additional bread, cheese, and dried meat to take with her.

As she was leaving, a commotion at the entrance attracted her notice. A young girl of about eleven turns was begging for food, and the tavern keeper was attempting to shoo her away. The child's drawn face tugged on Kira's heartstrings, and she slipped a black tile into the tavern keeper's hand.

"Get her something to eat, please."

The man gaped at the black tile. "This would feed the whole tavern."

"These are hard times. Just give the girl food and let her keep the change."

The child's eyes lit up as the tavern keeper crooked his

finger. "All right, then. Sit next to the kitchen and don't cause any trouble."

"Thank you," the girl replied.

Although Kira wasn't sure if the thanks were meant for her or the tavern keeper, she wasn't looking for gratitude. Perhaps absolution would be closer to the truth, since her conscience had been plaguing her since she'd fled the encampment. Mandral would likely seek retribution for her defiance—and the Nomads were now disarmed. Furthermore, who would make sure Dorsit drank grail mushroom tea in her absence? In the back of her mind, she also wondered if Mandral would send shadow hounds after her again. Her river crossing might confuse the magical creatures for a while, but they could pick up her scent eventually.

She scoured the town in search of supplies for the journey ahead. A horse and tackle were critical, along with a crossbow, hunting knife, water skin, and a thick blanket to guard against the nighttime chill. Several cygards were patrolling the main street but didn't glance at the woman passing by in a hooded cloak. The suns were setting, so she completed her purchases quickly. Spending the night in Addertown was, unfortunately, out of the question. Although her luck had been good thus far, she had no confidence it would remain so.

As twilight swept across the territory, Kira directed her sturdy mount deep into a forest several miles south of town, made camp, and strung her hammock between two trees. Exhausted from her long walk, she fell asleep almost immediately...and dreamed endlessly of Mandral.

SNAKE'S VENOM

Dorsit rode back from Mandral Village with the forged travel passes safely tucked into his pocket. To his chagrin, the process of obtaining the documents had taken a lot longer than he'd anticipated. Already citizens were finding ways to circumvent Mandral's iron-fisted rule, and he was not the first in line for an unauthorized travel pass. The scribe confided to him that he'd made a small fortune from his illicit activities but would soon be moving to the next village to avoid being caught.

While the wizard waited for the documents to be prepared, he visited the tavern and shopped at the bazaar. Ever since Mandral had imposed a heavy tax on commerce, the prices of everything had gone up. Under Nomad rule, people had been encouraged to enjoy the fruits of their labor, but no longer. Had he been able to work a few spells, he could have bartered for his purchases. He attempted an everlasting orb for Orly the tavern keeper, but the resulting ball of light was so small and weak he gave it to the man without asking anything in return. Still, his supply of gemstones worked as currency with most merchants, all of whom were unwilling to snitch on him to the roaming squads of cygards terrorizing the populace.

After the documents were ready, Dorsit left the village and headed back to the Nomad encampment. Although he and Kira had discussed leaving that day, because the hour had grown late, their departure would be delayed until the following morning. As he rode deeper into the forest, he began to notice outlying tents had disappeared, leaving the forest floor bare in large round spots. To his bewilderment, the entire Nomad encampment was gone. Only the tent he been assigned to remained, along with the wooden stable and a privy. A horse was tethered near the stable, and as he rode up, a young man emerged.

"What's going on, Arti?" Dorsit dismounted. "Where has everyone gone?"

"The Nomads have scattered. Chief Szul has offered you a place with us, if you wish."

When Arti described what had happened earlier than day with the cygards, Dorsit was immediately seized with worry for Kira.

"We can head north to the refuge caves," Arti concluded. "Or I'll accompany you to Ylan if you would prefer to go home."

Dorsit shook his head in disbelief. "What about Kira?"

"Her father believes she will not return here until it is time for her to fulfill her contract with Mandral."

Although he was in shock, Dorsit forced himself to consider his options. Had Kira abandoned their travel plans and fled to the refuge caves? If so, he should go with Arti and join her there. It was entirely possible, however, she intended to complete the journey to Mirrum Mountains alone. *If I know Kira, she would choose a quest, however arduous, over retreat.* He was too frail to travel alone, but could he attempt to transport to the Mirrum Mountains? When he remembered his pathetic efforts with a simple everlasting orb that morning, his heart sank.

"Thank you, Arti, but I'll remain here," he said finally.

"How will you survive on your own?"

"I have enough resources to support myself. I suspect Kira has undertaken a long journey, and I wish to be here for her when she returns."

"Consider your safety. Nomads won't be around to protect you."

"Since I resemble a decrepit old hermit, I doubt I pose a threat to the cygards. Nor do I present an attractive target for a thief."

Although Arti was reluctant to leave, Dorsit gave him no choice. After his friend rode off into the forest, Dorsit reluctantly brewed a pot of grail mushroom tea. As he sipped the concoction, he heard the clanking sound of armor outside. When he emerged, he discovered his tent was surrounded by scores of cygards, torches in hand. He lifted his arms in a helpless shrug.

"If you're looking for Nomads, they aren't here any longer."

"Where'd they go?"

"I don't know. I went into town this morning and when I returned, they'd disappeared." He shook his head, feigning sadness. "I can't believe they left an old man to fend for himself."

The cygards exchanged glances with one another, muttering amongst themselves.

"Gah! I wanted to burn something," one muttered in disappointment.

"Isore will be angry."

"Never mind Isore. It's the warlord you have to worry about."

Their conversations faded as they stomped toward the main road, and Dorsit's shoulders relaxed. He returned to his tent and downed his tea as if it were medicine. Perhaps he could recover enough strength to send a courier bird to the Mirrum Mountain nymphs, asking them to be on the lookout for a beautiful Nomad warrior.

~

IN THE MIDDLE of the night, Kira's eyes flew open. She sat up, listening intently for whatever had aroused her from a deep sleep. The call of a night bird. The creak of a tree branch as it swayed in the wind. A cricket. Just when she decided she'd been dreaming, a distant howl reached her ears. Not the bay of a shadow hound…but something sinister, nevertheless. Obviously Patnik had conjured another magical tracking creature to follow her. The time for rest was over.

As quickly as possible, she slid from her hammock and packed up her things. She'd just put her foot in the stirrup when another noise became audible…a child's whimpering cries. The child was running toward her through the woods, making no effort to mask his or her progress. Kira hid behind a tree, hunting knife at the ready. Less than a minute later, a young girl staggered past—the little beggar from Addertown.

When Kira reached out to grab the child's sleeve, she screamed and tried to twist away.

"Hey, I'm not going to hurt you!" Kira exclaimed. "I'm only trying to help!"

Overhead, the cloud cover moved away from the moons. As the moonlight filtering through the trees lifted the darkness, the child stopped her frantic efforts to free herself.

"You're that pretty lady who bought my dinner!"

"Why are you so far from town?"

The girl dragged a ragged sleeve across her face to mop her streaming nose and eyes.

"I don't have a home since the cygards came and killed my parents. And I'm running from the monster."

The eerie howl rang out again, more loudly than before. Kira's initial instinct was to hunt down whatever creature was howling and shove her knife between its ribs. Since she couldn't really assess the threat properly in the dark, however, she decided to keep moving southwest. If she were still being pursued at daybreak, she could take the creature's measure and decide how best to attack it then. First, however, she had to get the child to safety.

"Do you have any relatives nearby?"

"No. I don't have anyone to take care of me anymore."

Frustration. I can't leave her alone in the forest, especially now that she's covered with my scent. "What's your name?"

"Astral."

"All right, Astral. You can ride with me for a little while."

Kira lifted the child into the saddle and began to lead her horse through the forest by its bridle.

"Where are we going?" Astral asked.

"I have some cousins in Cheernaught who might be able to take you in."

Although she hadn't planned to stop at Cheernaught, it wasn't too much of a detour. *I need to purchase supplies for my ride into the mountains anyway, so this inconvenient development works in my favor.* Immediately she chastised herself for thinking of the child as an inconvenient development. Astral was helpless, and any Nomad would make sure she was protected, despite the personal cost. *I must make sure I don't lose my humanity while pursuing this quest. Otherwise I might save Dorsit and free myself from Mandral at the cost of my soul.*

Over the next few hours of darkness, Kira led her horse through the woods, pausing every so often to listen for the howl of Patnik's latest tracker. The creature seemed to be keeping pace, neither dropping back nor coming closer. Astral stayed awake for a while, but then her head drooped down until her chin was resting on her chest. Kira looped a rope around the child's waist and tied it onto the pommel to prevent her from falling off.

As the first of Yden's two suns lit the eastern horizon, Kira began to search for a good strategic spot to make her stand. As she passed into a clearing, she untied Astral and woke her. The child's eyes flew open.

"I need you to keep riding south. I'm going to stay behind and kill the monster. If all goes well, I'll catch up."

A crease formed between Astral's eyes. "What if it doesn't go well?"

"Ride to Cheernaught, find the Teryn family, and tell them Kira sent you. They won't turn you away."

"That's your name—Kira?"

"Yes."

"The monster won't be easy to destroy."

"Maybe not, but I've no choice." With every passing second, the sky was growing brighter. Kira lifted her weapons from the horse's saddle and gave Astral a nod. "Go on, then. I'll catch up as soon as I can."

A sharp slap on the horse's rump sent her off into the woods. Satisfied the child was out of harm's way, Kira loaded her crossbow with a metal-tipped dart and took cover behind a tree. As she waited for the monster to appear, her eyelids grew heavy. Her lack of sleep had begun to take its toll on her body, but she forced herself to stay alert.

A thick morning mist lent the clearing a ghostly appearance. When Mandral stepped out from the forest, the hair on Kira's arms stood on end. As he moved into the center of the clearing, the mist swirled around him like a mantle.

"Kira, my love, I can sense you're near. Come to me."

His voice caressed her skin like warm, fragrant oil, but the sensation was followed by a surge of fury. *He made me this way and deserves to suffer!* The crossbow fell to the ground and she drew her sword. *No silent dart for a clean kill; this is more personal.* With a loud warrior's cry, she sped from the shadows toward the man who'd poisoned her body and sapped her will. The handsome warlord smiled in welcome and spread his muscular arms wide. Confusion filled her mind and her pace slowed. *How can I cut down such a beautiful man?* Kira shook herself. *Because he's a wicked murderer! Strike now and be freed of him!* Her sword swung overhead in a mighty arc, but as the blade descended, she froze. *I can't hurt Mandral. I love him too much.*

"This isn't love," she whispered. "It's snake's venom."

"Give me a kiss," he urged.

"Never." But even as she spoke, Kira drove the sword into the soil and slumped to the ground in defeat. A sob welled up from the depths of her soul and tears poured from her eyes. Mandral reached for her just as a metal-tipped dart flew through the air and pierced his throat. With a gurgling cry, the warlord exploded into dust and disappeared.

"Wh-What?"

Astral ran over, Kira's crossbow in her hand. "That was an evil, shape-shifting jinn, conjured by a wizard. You're lucky it didn't touch you or you would've been enthralled."

Kira dropped her face in her hands. "I'm already enthralled."

Never before had she felt so inadequate or lost. The only skill she possessed was combat and even that had deserted her when it mattered most. *I'm not capable of protecting myself, much less anyone else.*

"You shouldn't have come back. As long as you're with me, you're in danger."

"I don't think so. Who was that man?"

"Warlord Mandral." Shame warmed her face. "He poisoned me with a potion that has no antidote."

"If you're fleeing from him, you must have some hope?"

"Perhaps. After I take you to Cheernaught, I'm heading into the Mirrum Mountains. I must seek help for a friend of mine from the nymphs who live there. There is a slim possibility they can do something for me too."

"I'll go with you. I'm pretty good with this crossbow, and my father taught me how to hunt."

"The mountains are no place for a child."

Astral's shoulders slumped. "I understand. You don't want me around."

The girl's downcast expression reminded Kira how her own sister had always made her feel unwelcome.

"It's not that I don't want you around, but there are bad people after me and I'm concerned for your safety."

"The wizard who sent the jinn won't send any more, if that's what you're worried about. It takes a lot of dark magic to conjure a jinn, so he'll be quite weakened for a while."

"Really? How do you know so much about magic?"

"Many turns ago, my father was a scribe. He learned a great deal about magic in his duties, but his opinion of wizards wasn't high."

"I've only ever known one wizard well, but he's a very good person. Nevertheless, I'd much rather wield a Nomad's sword than work magic. At least with a Nomad you always know where you stand."

The suns were well up in the sky, and Kira's stomach had begun to growl. Astral must have been hungry too because she folded her arms across her stomach and groaned.

"There's food in the saddlebags and my water skin is full," Kira said. "We should eat breakfast and then continue our journey. We've two days ride yet before we reach Cheernaught."

"You won't change your mind about bringing me to the mountains?"

"No. You belong with a family, Astral. With my cousins, you'll sleep in a real bed and eat regular meals. Where I'm going, I can't guarantee anything."

THE CASTLE'S newly completed throne room had been constructed with a tall cathedral ceiling and a series of windows down one side. A raised dais and blood red velvet curtain at the far end accentuated the heavy wooden chair from which the warlord would rule. Impressive artwork graced the walls, hung in between torches. Patnik and Tyrg stood off to one side while Mandral inspected the room.

"What is your opinion, Warlord?" Patnik asked.

Mandral cast a critical eye at the torches lighting the space. "It needs an everlasting orb."

The wizard's eyebrows drew together. "I'll conjure you an everlasting orb…as soon as I am able."

"What does that mean?"

"The dark magic with Kira has strained me more than I would have anticipated. I need a little time to recover."

Mandral gave Patnik a level glance. "How much time?"

The wizard gulped. "I-I should be able to conjure the orb by morning."

"See that you do, or it will be the worse for you."

Patnik sat down at one of the many trestle tables in the room and rested his head in his hands.

Tyrg cleared his throat. "Captain Isore has arrived to make his report, Warlord."

"Bring him to me and let him speak."

While he took his place on his throne, Mandral listened to Captain Isore's report.

"What do you mean the Nomads *disappeared?*" he asked.

"I sent squads of cygards to burn the encampment as you ordered, but the Nomads had fled. The only person remaining was a useless old man."

"More than likely, Rampen Szul anticipated retribution from our illustrious and fierce warlord and had the intelligence to flee from his wrath." Tyrg gave Mandral a deferential bow.

"We must pursue them." Mandral's gaze slid to gaunt and gray wizard, whose eyes were half closed. "Patnik!"

The wizard flinched and shook himself awake. "Yes, Warlord?"

"Conjure a tracker."

Patnik made a whimpering noise deep within his throat. "Forgive me, but I require a few days to recover—a week at most—before I can work that sort of magic."

"When you entered my employ, you represented yourself as a first-class wizard."

"Indeed I am, Warlord, but I've been working night and day for months!"

"I'm beginning to think you're malingering."

The Turtle Clan wizard visibly bristled at the accusation. "I can assure you—"

"If Patnik is truly exhausted, his transporter cuff and clan ring can be easily removed," Tyrg interrupted. "The ancient magic of inseparability binds the wizard to his magical artifacts unless his magical energy diminishes to a certain level or he is dead."

Mandral lifted an eyebrow. "How do you know this?"

"Most scribes are well-versed in wizard lore," Tyrg replied. "Isore, remove his transporter cuff."

"What?" Patnik attempted to flee but the cygard captain blocked his path. With considerable effort, Isore wrenched the silvery transporter cuff from the wizard's wrist and tossed it onto the table.

"That was wholly unnecessary, Warlord!" Patnik sputtered. "I've done all you've asked!"

"But what have you done for me lately?"

Mandral reached into his pocket, pulled out a fabric pouch, and poured the single gold coin contained therein into the palm of his hand. After he turned it over in his palm three times, the throne room echoed with the sound of a wizard's transport. When Efysian appeared, Patnik gave Mandral a wounded look, snatched up his transporter cuff, and strode from the room.

The Wolf Clan wizard smiled. "You sent for me, Warlord?"

"I need an everlasting orb suitable to light this chamber. And I need to be able to watch my enemies."

"These things come at a cost."

"Tyrg will pay what you ask. Oh, and can you conjure something to cover that bald pate of his? The shine is distracting."

"It would be my pleasure."

In the village of Derndale, Kira and Astral stopped at a tavern for food. The child ate more than Kira would have thought possible, given her small size.

"How can you hold so much?"

The girl giggled. "It's just so good. I'm not used to eating food."

"Do you mean you haven't eaten regularly?"

"That's right…not since my parents were killed."

While Astral finished her meal, Kira gazed out the window, deep in thought. Although the jinn had been eliminated, whatever creature was tracking her had not. The distant howling at night had continued to keep pace, allowing her scant few hours of rest. The lurking danger was like an itch she couldn't scratch, and the only way to assuage her anxiety was to keep moving. It wasn't in her nature to flee, but the creature seemed to be in no hurry to attack. As a result, she'd begun to question her decision to leave Astral in Cheernaught. To do so would not only place the child at risk, but her cousins as well. Furthermore, Derndale marked a decent route leading directly into the mountains. If she took the turnoff, she might be able to arrive in Mirrum within days.

Astral gave her a puzzled glance. "What's wrong?"

Kira realized she'd been frowning. "I'm sorry. Nothing's wrong, exactly, but I'm trying to decide the best course of action."

She flagged down the serving girl. "Excuse me, but where is the trail through the mountain pass? We're trying to get to Mirrum Village."

"The trailhead is on the south side of town. There's a narrow trail winding up the side of the mountain which goes through Mirrum Village, but it's a five-day ride."

The woman headed off to deliver her tray of mugs to a table full of prospectors, but Kira was distracted by movement outside the window. Not more than fifteen feet away, a squad of cygards had marched into Derndale from the south. Astral followed her gaze and gasped. They were trapped.

HUNTED

andral's tracker was hard on Kira's heels and now she was hemmed in by cygards. Even if the armored giants weren't looking for her specifically, neither she nor Astral had travel permits. Furthermore, her horse was tied up outside the tavern, right under the cygards' noses. Even if they escaped notice by slipping out the back of the building, they couldn't get far without the supplies in the horse's saddlebags. At the moment, however, she had a more immediate worry. The cygards had fanned out and were entering businesses along the main street, demanding to see travelers' permits. The tavern would be next.

Kira dropped a red tile down on the table to pay for the meal. "Let's go."

"How are we going to escape?"

"I don't know. We'll slip out the back and strategize later."

Astral grabbed Kira's wrist before she could move. "I'll get the horse and meet you on the trail."

"You don't have a travel permit. You'll be arrested as a vagrant!"

"I'm a child, remember? The cygards always ignored me in Addertown."

"I can't take that risk!"

"You don't have a choice."

Cygards were on the way into the tavern, and Kira could argue no longer. She hastened off, startling the tavern's cook as she fled through his kitchen and into an alley. Her dark green travel cloak billowed out behind as she darted into the adjacent woods. Although she waited for signs of pursuit, none were forthcoming. Despite her seemingly successful escape, she couldn't stop worrying about Astral. Could the child transact her business and be allowed to leave town without arousing suspicion?

In addition, Kira faced another challenge. The Mirrum Mountains were to the west, so she would have to cross the main street—now infested with Mandral's army—to get to the trail. Since the cygards had entered Derndale from the south, Kira guessed they'd already posted a checkpoint on that side of town. Her only chance would be to cross the road to the north, and double back through the woods. Nomad skills allowed Kira to run almost noiselessly through the forest. She kept the main road in sight, reaching the last outlying building just as the cygards finished setting up a roadblock into Derndale. A mile later, she encountered a wagon and driver on his way into town, raising a dust cloud on the dirt road in his wake. Kira took advantage of the billowing dirt and used it to shield her sprint to the west side of the road. No howling tracking creature had leaped on her in the process, and now all that remained was to find the trail into the mountains and hope Astral was not prevented from joining her.

～

To combat his isolation during Kira's absence, Dorsit rode into Mandral Village nearly every day. Under the warlord's regime, the village had changed rapidly. Commerce at the marketplace continued to flourish, but several unsavory merchants had joined the mix, including one who was rumored to trade in stolen wizard artifacts. Residents who used to greet passersby with welcoming smiles now scowled and turned their backs. Cygards were a frequent sight as they made their tax-collecting rounds and tossed suspected scofflaws into the back of a closed cart for transportation to the castle. Fear seemed to be indelibly woven into the fabric of the community. People even regarded close acquaintances with brusque suspicion. If it weren't for Kira, Dorsit would have been tempted to travel back to Ylan. Perhaps the cygards had taken over that town by now, but at least he would have been among friends.

The warlord's edicts required people to wear head coverings according to their profession, but Dorsit had lost his wizard's cap long ago, during his ordeal with Efysian. Even if he hadn't, he no longer felt comfortable presenting himself as a wizard. Although the mushroom tea was sustaining him tolerably well, but he dare not work any magic. Given current events, he might need a burst of energy in an emergency, and it wouldn't do to expend his magical resources on shallow things. Instead of a head covering, he wore a traveling cloak, which met the letter of the law and afforded him privacy, when necessary.

The future was on Dorsit's mind a great deal. If, by some miracle, Kira returned with a cure for his condition, he yearned to take Warlord Mandral down. Such thoughts were sheer fantasy, of course, since the odds of his restoration were slim. He was useless to anyone, and whenever the realization hit him, his mood spiraled downward into hopelessness. In a way, he was glad Kira wasn't around to see his depression. Before he was drained, he'd dedicated himself to beautifying the world and spreading happiness. Now, it seemed, Yden had devolved into a mean and ugly planet, almost like Hell. Many people believed Hell to be a myth, but one of his cousins and her Leopard Clan wizard husband had fled to Yrth—the planet known as Hell— during the last Wizards War. At the time, Dorsit had been shocked his cousin Misa would willingly spend life on a planet without magic. How ironic, then, that his own existence on Yden was now singularly dreary.

Lunch that day was a bowl of soup at Hafne's food stall. The big man used to be good-natured, but his demeanor had changed along with everything else. Still, Hafne always kept abreast of the news, and didn't mind sharing it freely with Dorsit.

"I heard Mandral has allied himself with Efysian." Hafne set Dorsit's bowl down on the table in front of him.

"No good has ever come from contact with that murderous wizard." Dorsit blew on the hot liquid to cool it, but nothing would ever cool his desire to avenge himself again Efysian.

"Of that, I have no doubt."

"What about Patnik?"

"It seems Mandral's been pushing him too hard and he's exhausted. The warlord isn't happy with Patnik's work."

"The warlord is never happy," Dorsit muttered.

"True. And it's getting harder and harder to make a living."

The wizard noticed a young man of about sixteen turns wander past, a look of confusion on his face. It wasn't his expression that caught Dorsit's eye, however, but his unusual clothes. His pants had large pockets sewn on the outside, and his boots were of a strange white material with a cunning crisscrossed lacing on top. The black, collarless shirt he wore was fashioned of a smooth, thin fabric, and featured a design with the word Leopard misspelled as Leppard. Although Dorsit had no idea what a def leppard was, he opened his mouth to ask the strange boy about it. Before he could speak to him, the boy sank down on one of the bales of hay Hafne used as seating and mumbled something Dorsit didn't quite catch.

Unfortunately, Hafne's capacity for curiosity was limited. He took off his hat, threatened the boy, and demanded he move on. Although the boy seemed to snap out of his confusion long enough to make a retort, Dorsit took pity on him.

"Give the lad a break, Hafne. Can't you see he's not from around here?"

"Stay out of it, Dorsit."

After another hostile exchange, the boy put his hands on the table and stood. Sunlight glinted off the transporter cuff on his wrist. Hafne grabbed him by the shoulder. "That's a transporter cuff, boy. Which wizard did you steal it from?"

"I didn't steal it, it's mine!"

The boy wore a clan ring as well as a transporter cuff, Dorsit noticed. He *was* quite young to be a full-fledged wizard, so where had he come from, and why did he act so disoriented? His behavior and manner of speech were also quite unusual— and intriguing. Had he transported to Mandral Territory from another continent?

Keen to know the answers, Dorsit set down his bowl. "Excuse me, young wizard—"

"He's no wizard. Oi, cygards, I've collared me a thief!" Hafne waved at a pair of cygards drinking at the tavern booth nearby. "Over here!"

"Hush, Hafne." Dorsit kept his voice low. "Don't involve the cygards!"

Unfortunately, his admonition came too late. As the armored giants approached, the boy panicked. Unable to free himself, he punched the big man in the gut to loosen his grip and sped off into the marketplace.

"Wait!" Dorsit exclaimed.

With cygards in pursuit, however, he couldn't blame the young wizard for not lingering. He'd caught no more than a glimpse of his ring, but he could have sworn it was shaped in the head of a dragon. Since all but one of the Dragon Clan had died off long ago, such couldn't be the case.

Hafne jammed his hat back on. "I hope the cygards catch the little vagrant."

"I don't. That boy was a friendly wizard."

"You're daft. He didn't look like a wizard."

"Looks can be deceiving."

Although Dorsit wasn't a seer, he couldn't help but think the boy's sudden arrival in Mandral Village was significant in some fundamental way. Due to Efysian's string of killings, wizard sightings were rare these days, but the boy was proof he'd not completely succeeded in eradicating the species. A tiny flame of excitement was rekindled in his breast. Maybe there was hope for Yden after all!

CONCERNED SHE WOULD MISS ASTRAL, Kira made her way as quickly as possible through the forest. She skirted the town and cut diagonally toward the trail so she wouldn't emerge at a spot where she would be seen. The afternoon shadows had grown long by the time she found the trail. Although she searched for fresh horse tracks in the dirt, there were no indications the child had already passed by. When Kira moved down the trail for a better view of the town, a black bird circling overhead swooped down and alit on a branch. The creature fixed its beady eyes on her, but Kira had greater concerns than wildlife. Several hours had passed since Astral had agreed to meet her, yet the child wasn't here. Had she been found out and detained?

After Kira cleared a curve, a cygard checkpoint became visible at the trailhead. She gasped and ducked behind a tree, but fortunately the cygards' attention was fixed in the opposite direction. A small group of prospectors was arguing with the trio of giants and gesticulating toward the mountain, but the cygards wouldn't let them pass. Although she was too far away to hear the conversation, she guessed the men hadn't obtained travel permits. As she watched, one of the cygards punched the most voluble man on the side of his head. The poor fellow staggered to one side, dazed, and his companions scattered.

Astral appeared, riding Kira's horse past the fracas with an unconcerned expression. To Kira's amazement, the cygards barely spared the child a glance. The horse and rider proceeded at a leisurely walk up the trail, while the cygards hauled the hapless prospectors away. With her arms akimbo, Kira stepped out to meet Astral.

"I can't believe you did it!"

The child grinned. "You needed my help."

"So I did."

Kira started to put her foot in the stirrup, to settle herself behind Astral, but the girl suddenly frowned at pointed at the black bird.

"How long has that been there?"

"Almost since I stepped onto the trail, why?"

"It's a spyrrow—a magical spying bird which transmits images to a spyball. Somebody is watching you."

In one seamless motion, Kira unhooked the crossbow from the horse's saddlebag and shot a dart toward the spyrrow. Unfortunately, the creature launched itself into the sky before the missile could kill it. In the next moment, Kira swung up into the saddle and urged the horse into a gallop. Up ahead, oak branches intersected to form an arbor.

"The spyrrow may lose sight of us underneath that canopy of trees."

Beneath the concealing tree branches, Kira slung the crossbow across her back and eased the horse into a fast walk. The bird did not reappear, and the tension in her shoulders began to relax. "I think we're safe for now."

"The spyrrow is a very advanced bit of magic," Astral said. "It wasn't sent by the same wizard as before."

"Why do you say that?"

"The dark magic required to conjure a jinn will continue to diminish his power for another few days."

"Perhaps Mandral has found another wizard to do his bidding, although I can't imagine who. Wizards are becoming more and more scarce."

The trail began to climb up the side of the mountain, until they had a view of the town below. The trail narrowed as they continued to climb and as the light began to fade, a distant rhythmic clanking noise reached Kira's ears. She peered over her shoulder, but could see nothing through the dense trees.

Astral cocked her head. "Do you hear that? It sounds like metal."

Clanking metal...just like the cygards marching toward Ylan! Fear made Kira's mouth go dry as she realized squads of the giants were marching up the trail in pursuit. Mandral had used the spyrrow to find her, and there was no place to hide. With very little daylight left, she urged her horse to go faster.

"What's wrong?" Astral asked.

"Cygards. I'm going to ride until I can't see the trail and then lead the horse on foot, like I did in the forest. The cygards can't march all night, and we already have a good head start. Maybe we'll come across someplace to hide."

"There's an old mineshaft up ahead somewhere."

"How do you know?"

"The prospectors in the tavern were whispering about it. They'd discovered a deposit of gold and were replenishing their food supplies in Derndale before going back."

"I didn't hear any of that conversation."

"You were preoccupied."

"I was, rather." She'd become lost in a wistful daydream about Mandral, and had almost forgotten to eat.

"The shaft is so deep, it's rumored to lead directly to Mirrum Village."

"But that's the other side of the mountain!"

Astral shrugged. "I don't know if it's true or not, but the prospectors were eager to visit the nymphs."

"Unfortunately, the mineshaft will be dark as pitch and we don't have any lanterns to carry with us."

"We do now. I bought one, along with extra food and blankets."

"How did you get the money?"

"You paid for my dinner in Addertown with a black tile, remember? The tavern keeper gave me the change."

Kira felt a surge of affection for the child. "I'm glad you're here, Astral."

THE ENTRANCE to the mineshaft had been poorly concealed with cut tree branches, fortunately, so Kira found it easily, even as twilight faded to black. Astral produced the lantern, which produced an unusually steady light. In addition, the lantern was cleverly fitted with a metal cover to block the light when necessary.

"That's not like any oil lamp I've ever seen," Kira said.

"It contains a small everlasting orb."

"Those are extremely rare!"

"It cost me every bit of money I had, but it'll be worth it. It might take us days to get through the mineshaft, and an oil lamp would burn out."

Kira removed the saddle, blanket, and bridle from the mare and sent her up the trail with a smack to her hindquarters. Hopefully, the cygards would continue to follow the horse's tracks and not think to look for her and Astral in the mineshaft.

While the girl waited inside the mineshaft with the saddlebags and supplies, Kira flung the saddle itself over the side of the mountain so it wouldn't be seen. As she backed away from the cliff, she paused to listen to the cygards' approach. Although the giants were still some distance away, they hadn't interrupted their pursuit for any length of time. Could they march without stopping until they reached Mirrum Village?

After concealing the mineshaft entrance more fully with leafy pieces of brush, Kira squeezed behind the foliage. The vertical shaft yawning ahead appeared to be a natural fissure in the rock, widened over time by the pickaxes of miners. A wheelbarrow had been left at the side of the entrance, presumably by the prospectors in Derndale. When Astral lifted the lantern closer, the tools stacked therein gleamed from the gold dust coating their surfaces.

Kira bent to pick up the saddlebags, groaning inwardly at their weight and bulk. Although Astral was carrying the lantern, Kira also allowed her to sling the crossbow on her back, as well as the new bedroll she'd purchased in Derndale.

"Let's get started. We need to put some distance between us and entrance or the cygards will see the light from the lantern," Kira said.

Astral grimaced, and she set out at a brisk pace. "Come on!"

An hour later, Kira's very bones were weary, and she began to look for a place where they could camp for the night. The shaft had remained straight and level, but the straps of her saddlebags were biting into her shoulders. They'd passed several niches, formed where veins of gold had been mined. At the next alcove, which was about half the size of the tent she'd shared with her sister, Kira lowered her bags to the ground.

"We should be safe in here for the night. Let's eat and get some rest."

Astral sighed with relief. "I'm so glad. I'm starving, and I can't take another step."

Kira had expected to dine on dried meat, but found freshly

baked chicken, bread, butter, and cheese packed inside the saddlebags instead, along with a stoppered bottle of tea.

"This is a feast!" she exclaimed. "You continue to amaze me, Astral."

The girl giggled, but said nothing because she was chewing on a piece of buttered bread. Kira ate until she was full, but Astral gorged herself until she couldn't take another bite. Kira gathered the bones in a napkin.

"When you're settled, I'm going to take these chicken bones back up the mine shaft and bury them in an alcove."

"Why not bury them here?"

"It's not a good idea. If there are any wild animals around, they'll smell the bones, and I don't want any nasty surprises in the night. Oh, and leave your shoes on, just in case."

Kira helped Astral get comfortable, and then brought the lantern with her as she sought a good place to leave the remains of their meal. After walking five minutes, she dropped the bones in an alcove and covered them with a number of rocks left over when the gold was extracted. Satisfied they wouldn't be attacked by bears, Kira returned to the campsite and settled down next to Astral. The child was snoring gently by the time she lowered the cover over the lantern. As Kira stared out into the darkness, she listened for any signs the cygards had entered the mineshaft. She heard nothing to alarm her and so allowed her eyes to close.

We're safe.

AS SHE SLID into Mandral's arms, his long black hair brushed against the skin of her cheek. Their lips met, but even as she surrendered to her emotions, something felt wrong. Puzzled, she pulled back.

"What is it, my love?"

Mandral's whisper made her shiver with delight. As he pulled her close once more, however, she had the sudden suspicion she was dreaming.

"This isn't real." She shook her head. "I must wake up."

"Our love only feels like a dream."

This time, Mandral's voice held an undercurrent of savagery. Kira glanced up at him, and gasped. His skin was covered with fur and he'd sprouted curly tusks from his mouth. As he grunted and bared his animal teeth, she fought to escape.

Wake. Up. Now.

As if a bucket of ice water had been thrown in her face, Kira woke. Although she was conscious, a slight disorientation remained, and it took a moment for her to remember she was in the mineshaft. Then she realized an animal's grunts and snuffling noises had forced her from slumber. As she reached for the knife in her boot, a powerful stench from the creature almost made her swoon. Although the scent was nothing she'd ever smelled before, the noxious mixture of mold, swamp gas, and rotting meat told her she was dealing with a vicious mountain troll. The snuffling grew closer, and Kira guessed the troll smelled the discarded chicken bones. Although the knife was in her hand at that point, she remained as still as death. If she and Astral were very, very fortunate, the troll would pass them by in favor of the bones. If not, she would die defending the child and hope the girl made it out of the mineshaft safely.

Kira's heart hammered in her ears as the troll stopped at their alcove and grunted. Trolls could see in the dark, so she knew the creature was aware of their presence. Nevertheless, she lay still and played dead. To her sweet relief, the troll moved on, snuffling as it tried to locate the greasy chicken carcass. She planned to wait until the creature was far enough past before grabbing Astral and bolting. Unfortunately, the child awoke, gasping for air.

"What's that awful smell?"

MIRRUM VILLAGE

When he heard Astral's voice, the troll roared with rage. Ill-prepared to fight in the dark, Kira fumbled for the lantern and lifted its cover. The naked troll, which had been inches away, recoiled. With the lantern in one hand and her knife in the other, Kira jumped from the alcove and prepared to battle.

"Run, Astral! Keep running and don't look back!" Kira cried.

With a high-pitched scream, Astral scrambled to her feet and disappeared from sight. Kira raised the lantern toward the troll and brandished her weapon. To her shock, the enormous creature stumbled backward, raising his lumpy hands in a defensive fashion, as if the light hurt his eyes. Kira was confused for a moment, until she made the connection; trolls turned to stone in the light of the suns. The illumination emitted by an everlasting orb simulated the brightness of sunlight, which made it the best weapon she had.

When the moss-covered troll swung his ham fist toward the light, Kira managed to pull the lantern out of the way. His other fist connected with her shoulder, unfortunately, and sent her flying. Her grip on the lantern loosened, and it slipped to the ground. The everlasting orb was dimmed as the cover dropped down, and the emboldened troll raised his calloused foot to crush Kira underneath. Dazed, she tried to roll out of the way, but if Astral had not picked up the lantern and lifted the cover, she would have been killed.

The troll bolted, but as Kira sat up, another strange sight came into view. In the far distance, bobbling torchlight was lighting the mineshaft, and a rhythmic metallic clanking noise echoed off the rock tunnel.

"The cygards found us!" Astral exclaimed.

"Let the troll deal with them."

"Is *that* what it was?" she shuddered. "I thought at first it was the howling monster, until I remembered we'd already killed the jinn."

Although a warm trickle down her neck meant her head was bleeding, Kira grabbed her weapons and saddlebags and prepared to flee.

This time we don't stop until we reach the other side.

Sounds of the battle between troll and cygards raged for a long time. Eventually, silence returned to the mineshaft, broken only by Kira's and Astral's footfall and occasional squeaks from the lantern handle.

"I can't believe we saw a troll and lived to tell about it," Kira said at last.

"Its skin was covered with moss and mold." A grimace. "I think trolls are uglier than anything."

"I won't think him quite so ugly if he stops the cygards from pursuing us."

"I'm sure he can, by smell alone."

Despite everything, Kira laughed.

"Do you suppose there are more trolls in the mine?" Astral asked.

"I can't promise anything, but trolls are usually solitary creatures. I suppose that explains why there are so few of them."

Several more hours passed, and Astral was finally unable to go another step. Kira paused their journey long enough for them both to drink and nibble some food, and then she carried the child piggyback. Although Astral wasn't heavy, Kira's muscles shook from fatigue. In addition, pain radiated from the cut on her head and the bruise to her shoulder. With no other choice, however, she continued to put one foot in front of the other.

"I think I see light," Astral said finally.

When Kira closed the cover on the lantern, a tiny pinprick of illumination was visible about a mile distant. Like a horse sensing water, a sudden surge of energy propelled her forward. She emerged from the mineshaft just as her strength gave way. After she put Astral down on her feet, Kira staggered over to the nearest tree and collapsed. Try as she might, she couldn't hold onto her consciousness. Moments later, she passed out.

~

"KIRA SZUL?"

"Wake up, Princess."

"Time to rise and shine!"

Puzzled at the sound of the familiar female voices, Kira opened her eyes. Somehow she'd been moved to a bed, inside a dwelling. Even more extraordinary, she was surrounded by the vibrantly colored nymphs, Elle, Glory, and Delphine.

"Where am I, and what are you doing here?" she exclaimed.

Giggles.

"You're in Mirrum Village," Elle said. "This is Lady Hightower's residence."

"Dorsit asked us to look for you," Delphine said. "He thought you might be coming this way."

"Why are *you* here?" Glory asked.

"I came to speak with the Mirrum Mountain nymphs, to see

if they could help Dorsit…and me." Kira sat up abruptly. "Is Astral safe?"

The nymphs exchanged pointed glances.

"Oh, she's fine."

"She eats like a puleden."

"Er…what do you know about her?"

"She's an orphan I met along the way, and I'm trying to take care of her." Kira glanced down at herself and gasped. Although she was covered by a sheet, she wore nothing else. The nymphs noticed her discomfiture and giggled.

"You were filthy, so we took the liberty of removing your clothes."

"Lady Hightower healed your injuries with some herbal compresses. You'd lost a lot of blood."

"Did you know you talk in your sleep?"

Kira's face burned with embarrassment—and a bit of resentment—knowing full well her secret had been inadvertently revealed.

The nymphs stood.

"Once you're dressed, Lady Hightower wants to see you."

"Please let her know cygards are chasing me. They might come here through the mineshaft tunnel."

"The what?"

"The mineshaft that burrows through the mountain."

Again, the nymphs exchanged glances.

"We'll let Lady Hightower know," Elle said finally.

After the nymphs sauntered out of the room, Kira threw back the sheet and stretched. Other than a little soreness in her muscles, she felt surprisingly good. Her skin, hair, and fingernails were fresh and clean, and someone had even thought to buff and file her broken nails into shining ovals. She didn't know how she could be clean without having taken a bath, but she supposed amongst water nymphs, anything was possible.

The feeling of fresh clothes against her skin was also

remarkably pleasant, but shortly after she'd dressed, a powerful thirst and hunger drove her from the room, in search of a meal. When she emerged onto an open catwalk, an awesome view awaited her. Lady Hightower's house had been built on the side of the mountain, and an amazing tree-filled vista spread out like a green, wooly carpet as far as the eye could see. Kira peeked over the railing, but saw nothing below but the mountainside. Apparently, the house was cantilevered off the slope, held up by stilts.

She followed the catwalk past several closed doors—bedrooms she assumed—until she reached the double doors leading into the common dwelling. Astral was sitting at a table covered with food, eating breakfast. Her former ragged dress had been replaced with a tunic and full pants fashioned of cerulean silk, and her soft, clean hair was tied back with a ribbon. Although the girl was occupied with her meal, she did wave when Kira appeared.

A handsome nymph, who was draped in a silken robe of creamy white, greeted Kira with a smile. The woman's smooth light brown skin was beautifully contrasted with her light green eyes, and her braided hair was twisted into a large topknot and held in place by a polished twig.

"I'm Lady Hightower, the leader of Mirrum Village. You are very welcome here." Her musical voice reminded Kira of a wooden flute. "Sit down and refresh yourself. I'm certain you must be hungry after your journey."

Kira's stomach contracted with hunger as she regarded the repast, but she had another concern.

"Before I do anything else, I must warn you about Warlord Mandral's cygard army. They may follow me here, and I don't want to place any of you in danger."

Lady Hightower was not too dignified to giggle.

"There's no danger, I can assure you, but thank you for your concern." She gestured to the table. "Eat first. We'll talk later."

The nymph disappeared, and Kira helped herself to breakfast. Some of the food was familiar, like eggs, but a tender griddle cake served with hot syrup was new and delicious. Astral wiggled with delight. "Isn't it good?"

"It *is* good. I'm glad we're here." Kira chewed a bite of griddle cake, letting the sweet syrup explode on her tongue.

"The whole village is built on the side of the mountain, and all the houses are connected by little bridges and ladders. I was scared to go near the railings at first."

"What happened after I passed out?"

"I ran to the village for help and they brought you here. You were very pale."

"I hope I didn't frighten you too much."

Astral searched her face. "After everything that's happened, you're worried about me?"

"It's only natural. You're a child." Kira paused. "When we return to my home, would you like to stay with us? I'm sure my father won't mind, and you'll be as safe with the Nomads as you would be anywhere else."

The child's eyes grew watery. "I'd like that very much."

"It's settled, then."

Three griddle cakes later, Kira pushed her plate away, but Astral managed to finish the entire platter. As soon as she finished the last one, Lady Hightower appeared.

"The water nymphs from your territory brought me a letter from the wizard Dorsit, asking me to render you aid," she said. "How may I help?"

"Dorsit has been drained of his life energy and has grown old before his time. To your knowledge, is there anything that can help restore his youth?"

"He mentioned you'd been poisoned by the warlord Mandral."

Kira averted her gaze. "Yes. I would be greatly in your debt if you had a remedy."

"A ginbush grows on this mountain, which produces enough berries to help only one of you, I'm afraid. It might cure your poisoning, but I can't know for certain. For Dorsit it would boost his magical energy only a little. You must choose."

Disappointment followed Lady Hightower's reply, but the choice seemed clear. The ginbush berries might help her, but they might not. If she ate the berries, she might condemn Dorsit to an early death and still not solve her problem.

"I'll take the berries to Dorsit. As long as he's alive, there's hope for a cure."

Astral gaped. "I would have chosen the opposite way!"

"You don't know Dorsit the way I do," Kira said. "He's as dear to me as a brother. As to my condition, I'll have to find another solution."

Lady Hightower picked up Kira's teacup. At the bottom, only tea leaves remained. The nymph peered at the leaves, as if something were written there.

"The only certain cure for a love potion is true love. You will meet such a man soon."

"If I'm to fall instantly in love with a stranger, I'm not interested. I've had enough of such emotions."

"True love doesn't work that way. Lasting love takes time to develop, and you always have choices. My advice to you is to accept the gift of freedom from Mandral's poison, and to let your relationship with this stranger grow over time, as it will. Love between humans often takes a circuitous path." Lady Hightower giggled. "Odd advice from a nymph, to be sure."

Although Kira was dubious about anything gleaned from tea leaves, she didn't want to be rude. "Thank you, Lady Hightower. If you'll show me where to collect the berries, I'll trouble you no further. And is there anyone from whom I could purchase a horse? Astral and I must get back to Dorsit as quickly as possible, and I don't wish to take the mineshaft route again."

A furrow appeared on Lady Hightower's brow. "Elle mentioned something about that earlier. There's no such route."

"Forgive me, but Astral and I traversed it ourselves, and nearly got killed by a mountain troll!"

The nymph's gaze slid to Astral and a serene smile lifted the corner of her lips. "I'm certain everything will be made clear to you in due course. And I believe transportation has already been arranged."

The woman dissolved into mist and disappeared. Kira blinked as she realized a glass jar had materialized next to her plate. Closer examination revealed a handful of small dried berries inside.

"I suppose this is what I came for." She stood. "I'll get my things and we'll go."

Glory, Delphine, and Elle ran into the room. Each nymph wore only a tiny sarong tied around their hips, and a necklace fashioned of acorns and polished stones.

"We're here to escort you back to the trail," Glory said.

Delphine flicked a glance at Astral. "You and *her.*"

"Give our best to Dorsit." Elle sighed. "That wizard used to be so handsome!"

"You're not going to return with us?" Kira asked.

"Not while Mandral and the cygards are there!" Glory said.

"Besides which, we like living in Mirrum Village," Delphine said. "It's kind of nice not having men around."

"For a little while, at least," Elle added.

Glory giggled. "A *very* little while."

Peals of laughter rang out. Inwardly, Kira rolled her eyes.

Kira gathered her belongings, making sure to wrap the jar of berries in a blanket so it wouldn't get broken on the journey home. As she donned her traveling cloak, she snorted with derision at Lady Hightower's prediction. Even if she were to meet a man she could love forever, it didn't necessarily follow the man would love her in return. Before the invasion, her notions of romance had been wistful fancies dreamed up by a naïve young girl. Now, she viewed love with jaded suspicion. Perhaps her feelings would change if—no, *when*—she rid herself of her obsession with Mandral. She couldn't imagine they would.

The three nymphs led her and Astral through Mirrum Village, across a number of slender rope bridges and up several ladders. When they reached the road, to Kira's astonishment her mare awaited, equipped with the bridle and saddle she'd hurled off the side of the mountain. With her mouth open, Kira stared.

"What's wrong?" Delphine asked.

"Never seen a horse before?" Elle asked.

"That bewildered expression isn't your best look, Princess," Glory said.

Astral nudged Kira in the ribs. "Just go with it. As Lady Hightower said, it'll all be clear soon."

"I hope so. I'm beginning to believe I'm out of my senses," Kira replied.

She lifted Astral into the saddle and settled behind her.

"Good-bye, nymphs," Kira said. "Thank you for your help."

The triad waved cheerily. "Good-bye and good luck!"

Kira took the reins of her horse and nudged her forward. The wide path was on a gentle downward slope, and the weather was good. The server in Derndale had mentioned the route would be a five-day ride, unless she encountered cygards. Hopefully, the troll had taken care of that particular threat, but the spyrrow might return and alert Mandral to her position again. Somehow she would have to circumvent the cygards' checkpoints, so it might be ten days before journey's end.

Ten minutes later, they approached a gnarled tree at a bend in the road. Kira recognized the distinctive tree immediately. After emerging from the mineshaft, she'd collapsed underneath its stippled blossoms. Strangely enough, however, when the horse rounded the bend, no tunnel opening appeared in the smooth rock face. Assuming she'd misjudged the distance, Kira rode on a little further, but saw nothing remotely resembling a mineshaft, tunnel, passageway, or even a dent in the mountain. Up ahead, however, the road ended at a sheeting waterfall. Kira reined in the horse.

"What's this?"

"Just ride through it," Astral said. "Lady Hightower told me it's how she keeps the village secret."

"Considering everything, I suppose this isn't the strangest thing that's happened of late."

Kira dismounted, took a deep breath, and led the horse underneath the smooth, flat plane of water at a run. When she emerged on the far side, she was beyond stunned.

"But...this is the field where you killed the jinn!"

She glanced up to get Astral's reaction, but the child was gone. No waterfall was visible, either, and it was as if neither had ever existed.

"Astral!"

In a panic, she left the horse grazing, and bolted toward the tree line. "Astral, where are you?"

The unearthly howl of the tracker came from mere yards away. She turned to see a woman in a blue silk tunic standing in the middle of the field—only she wasn't completely solid. Kira could see through her body to the forest beyond.

"Astral?"

A nod.

Kira gulped. "What are you?"

"I'm the jinn conjured by the wizard Patnik, only he didn't know exactly what he was doing. I'm not the sort of jinn to do any mortal's bidding, but I can't return to the spirit world without taking a soul."

"You could have taken my soul at any time. Why wait until now?"

"I'm not allowed to take the soul of a truly good person, so I needed time to test you. You acted in a noble fashion, always, and I'm humbled to make your acquaintance." A slight twinkle in the jinn's eyes reminded Kira of the child Astral. "And I very much enjoyed the food."

A sudden rush of emotion blurred Kira's vision. She'd come to view Astral almost like a younger sister. "So you're leaving?"

"I feel no compunction about taking Patnik's soul. He knew the risk before he conjured me."

"I-I'll miss you."

In the next moment, young Astral was running toward her, as solid and winsome as ever. She wrapped her arms around Kira and gave her a hug. When she stepped back, her cheeks were wet with tears. "I'm not supposed to feel anything for humans." She drew her sleeve across her eyes. "I'm afraid I failed in that regard."

"Are you sure you can't stay?"

"I wish I could, but I've already stayed too long."

Astral sprinted off, disappearing before she'd reached more than a few yards. A keen pang of loneliness descended. Kira sat down on a nearby log and sobbed.

As MANDRAL ATE a sumptuous lunch in the throne room, the spyrrow chirped in his cage nearby.

Tyrg appeared. "Warlord, the wizard Patnik has been found dead in his chambers."

A sound of disgust. "Pity. I would have liked to kill him myself and make a public event of it." He shrugged. "Now that the spyrrow has shown me where the Nomads are hiding, it's of little consequence. We can always summon Efysian to fulfill our needs from now on."

"Yes, Warlord."

"Have we any news from the cygards in pursuit of the princess?"

"Er...only two returned to Derndale. The others followed Kira into a mineshaft and perished at the hands of a troll."

"Then she is likely dead as well."

"Her sixteenth birthday is in two days. If she doesn't present herself for the wedding, I believe we may safely assume she is dead. A Nomad's word is binding."

"If she doesn't appear, I'll wed her by proxy. It's imperative I be seen as Chief Szul's lawful heir."

"I'll begin making the arrangements."

"Tyrg, I wish to begin holding court. Invite our wealthiest neighbors to visit and direct the cygards to bring me prisoners every afternoon so I may pass judgment."

"And if we don't have any prisoners?"

"Any pretext will do. It's time to have a little pageantry...and fun."

HAPPY RETURNINGS

The Nomad encampment was only a day's ride away, and since Kira knew where the cygard checkpoints were, she managed to successfully avoid them. At Addertown, she sold her mare back to the stable owner, and paid the ferryman to take her across the river. During the long walk to the Nomad encampment, her apprehension increased. Would she discover Mandral had killed her father and slaughtered the Nomads in retribution for her defiance? It was small satisfaction that the wizard Patnik would be dead by now, since Mandral had already allied with another wizard. Could she carry out the warlord's assassination with the effects of the poison still running through her veins? She had no choice but to succeed.

Kira entered the grail mushroom field, anticipating a Nomad escort as soon as she was spotted. To her dismay, none appeared. Fearing the worst, she entered the forest. Soon, it became clear the encampment was gone. Although the central wooden pavilion remained, the tent dwellings had been removed. As she peered through woods, she spied one lone tent. With her heart in her throat, she sped down the path. "Dorsit!"

The wizard emerged from the dwelling and peered in her direction. "Kira?"

Careful not to knock the frail man down by an overly enthusiastic greeting, she embraced him. "I'm so glad to see you. Where has everyone gone?"

"As far as I know, the Nomads are alive—including your father."

Kira bit back tears of relief.

"Come inside for some delicious grail mushroom tea." Dorsit rolled his eyes. "A great many things have happened during your absence."

"I've much to tell you, too."

Over the tea, Dorsit recounted his conversation with Arti. Kira nodded when he mentioned her father's plan to split the Nomads into groups until they could rebuild their weapons.

"Yes, I've seen the retreat caves before. So now the Nomads are split in half and virtually defenseless?" She sighed. "At least they are alive."

In turn, she related her adventures on her journey to Mirrum Village. When she told him about the jinn, Astral, he gasped with horror.

"Patnik is a fool to be dabbling in that sort of black magic!"

Kira shook her head. "I daresay he's paid the ultimate price for having done so, but Mandral won't care. He's already allied himself with another wizard, although I don't know who."

She produced the jar of berries. "Lady Hightower sent these to you, to boost your energy. I'm afraid she did not have a cure, but we'll continue to look."

"And did she have a remedy for you?"

On her trek home, Kira had thought long and hard about what to tell Dorsit. If he knew she was still debilitated, he would try to stop her from going to Mandral.

"Yes," she lied. "She gave me a purifying water to drink, but I won't be completely cured of my nightmares until the warlord is dead."

"I'm so relieved. Tomorrow is your birthday, have you forgotten?"

"I thought I had another few days!" She averted her eyes. Only one night remained until she had to execute her plan.

Dorsit seemed to read her thoughts. "I won't let you go to the castle. The contract is a fraud."

"Yes, but you can tell no one about the poison. You promised!"

"I'll keep my promise, of course, but I still have the forged travel permits. We should travel to the retreat caves tomorrow to speak with your father. It's possible he's devised some plan of attack."

She nodded in agreement, even though she intended no such thing.

"I need a mount. Why don't you go into the village tomorrow to purchase one? The cygards will be looking for me, so I'll stay here, out of sight."

"I'll go right after breakfast." He paused. "There's something else you should know. I've seen a young wizard in the village, and he doesn't look like he's from around here."

"Is he Mandral's new alliance, do you think?"

"Since he ran from the cygards, definitely not. I haven't seen him since, but I have the feeling his presence here is significant."

"In what way?"

"My clan ring didn't alert me to the presence of a hostile wizard, so that means he's not aggressive. Also, it's rather exciting to know Efysian missed a wizard. Perhaps there are more of them where this boy came from."

"Does this wizard have a name?"

"I'm sure he does, but I just don't know it yet."

Kira still had provisions left over from her journey, so as she and Dorsit prepared something for the evening meal, she pondered what he'd said. Although her respect for him was immense, he'd always had a tendency toward dreaminess. He might consider the young wizard significant, but she had her doubts. Besides which, any assistance the lad could offer would arrive too late for her. As soon as Dorsit had departed for Mandral Village the following morning, she would head for the castle. Despite her resolution to assassinate the warlord, she suspected her plan—even if successful—would end with her death.

EARLY THE FOLLOWING MORNING, Dorsit left Kira at the encampment while he rode into town. Not only did he intend to purchase a horse, but he hoped to find her a birthday present as well. When he arrived, he bypassed a booth displaying a tempting array of ribbons and jewelry. The booth was owned by Moala the merchant, who was an unsavory character by anyone's reckoning. Because of Kira's interest in lotions and perfumes, he purchased a set of essential oils at Marybell's booth instead.

As Dorsit headed for the stables, he began to feel faint from the heat of the day. He detoured inside the tavern tent for a drink. Although the presence of two cygards wasn't enough to dissuade him from ordering a beverage, he did step outside the tent to drink it. After the refreshing ale slid down his throat, he felt much better. A young man was walking in his direction, slipping and sliding on the muddy road. Although he was wearing the hat and clothes of a lackey, his bearing was not that of a servant. A sudden shaft of excitement shot through Dorsit as he realized the wizard had returned.

Inside the tavern tent, however, the cygards had finished their ale and they were about to emerge. When Dorsit finally caught the young wizard's eye, he attempted to wave him off.

The boy lifted his hand in acknowledgment, but then the cygards blocked Dorsit's line of sight. After the giants moved past, the boy had disappeared. He couldn't have transported away, because Dorsit would have heard it, but where had the young wizard gone? How disappointing if he were to miss him a second time!

Dorsit crossed the street to search for him in the marketplace, but several minutes later he heard a fracas at Moala's tent. When the cygards dragged the boy into view, Dorsit opened his mouth to speak. After the cygard growled in his direction, however, Dorsit became worried he would make the lad's situation worse and said nothing. The cygards dragged the boy toward a prisoner cart, at which point he really struggled to free himself.

"This is all a misunderstanding. I'm a wizard and it's my cuff!"

In the next moment, one of the cygards hit the young wizard with his metal prod and knocked him unconscious. The boy's limp form was tossed into the cart, and as Dorsit watched the cart drive off, a feeling of self-loathing took over. The loss of his magical abilities was painful, but the loss of his manhood was worse. He'd been forced to stand by like an old woman while the cygards had bullied the boy, and he couldn't lift a finger to intercede.

I'm useless.

∼

ON THE MORNING of her birthday, Kira woke up with a sick feeling in the pit of her stomach. She squeezed her eyes shut and let fear consume her for a few moments before shaking it off and rising to meet the day's challenge. *A warrior of only sixteen turns is quite young to die, but since the mission is righteous, my death will be a good one.*

Dorsit had also risen early and was making tea. "Many joyful returnings, Kira."

"Thank you, Dorsit."

After the Leopard Clan wizard departed for Mandral Village, she scribbled a note, explaining where she'd gone and why. Then, she prepared herself for the task at hand. Because any visible weapons would be confiscated at the castle, she left her sword at camp. Instead, razor-sharp stilettos were secreted inside the tops of both boots, and a lethal throwing knife was hidden in a holster underneath her arm. She'd be wearing a traveling cloak and a besotted smile, so the weapons would be overlooked.

The day had grown quite warm when she left the tent, so she took the shortest route to the main road. Fortunately, she managed to catch a ride with a farmer making a delivery to the castle. Bushel baskets of vegetables and grains filled the back of the wagon, and she asked the farmer if there was some special occasion planned.

"The Nomad princess is supposed to arrive today for her upcoming wedding to the warlord. If not, there's to be a wedding in proxy, I'm told." He shrugged. "Either way means a celebration."

So she was to be wedded to the warlord whether or not she was present? Although the concept disgusted her, Mandral was within his legal rights under the contract of engagement to marry her by proxy. His timely death at her hands, however, would constitute withdrawal of consent.

The farmer let her off at the access road used for deliveries, and she continued on by foot to the main entrance where cygards were posted.

"Take me to Warlord Mandral," she demanded.

Their laughter had a muffled, hollow sound inside their metal helmets.

"Mandral is expecting me. I'm Kira Szul."

Her statement had a galvanizing effect on the giants, and they scrambled to open the gates.

"This way, Princess."

Flanked on either side by clanking cygards, Kira strode up the long driveway toward the castle. As she rounded a slight bend, the edifice loomed into view. Bleak and cold, the gray granite castle reminded her of Mandral's heart. Sharp spires scraped the sky, as if doing battle with nature itself, and the cygards roaming the grounds completed the picture of an impenetrable fortress. Her heart skipped a beat as she realized she would never emerge from the castle alive.

Despite its forbidding appearance, the castle had attracted a crowd that day. Expensive carriages lined the courtyard, and as Kira approached, she noticed an expensively clad couple ascending the steps. Was her marriage-by-proxy taking place at that very moment? A giddy feeling spread through her body, and suddenly she couldn't wait to see Mandral and call him her husband. At the thought of his tender embrace, a delicious shiver coaxed a smile to her lips. Passion sped her ascent into the castle. How soon could she be alone with her bridegroom?

Remember the poison.

No matter what she felt, and how ardently she yearned for Mandral, it was a lie.

Lies. All lies. Mandral brings nothing but death and destruction to everything he touches…including me.

Kira was absolutely determined to carry out the assassination—until a portrait of the warlord hanging in the castle entranceway made her catch her breath. His handsome face seemed to hold her heart in his hand. Perhaps she would live with him for a few days before killing him. More time was necessary for her to gather her resolve. She needn't kill him right away. Tears sprang to her eyes.

I cannot do it. I am undone.

A cygard put out his hand to stop her from entering the throne room.

"Your weapons, please."

She gestured toward the place on her belt where a sword would hang. "As you see, I'm unarmed."

"The warlord gave orders you were to be searched."

Rough hands grabbed Kira and searched her frame. Anger flared at the assault. Whatever tenderness she felt toward Mandral definitely didn't extend to his cygards, and when the giants discovered and confiscated her blades, her anger turned to rage. Despite his armor, her vicious sidekick to one of the cygard's knees made him howl with pain, even as another cygard managed to loop a rope around her wrist. As he hauled her into the throne room like an animal, Kira jammed a side-kick into his midsection. Bent double from the blow, he staggered down the aisle. A jumping, twisting hook kick sent the cygard's helmet flying off his head—exposing his oozing skin to the open air.

Mandral's voice rang out, laced with merriment. "Subdue our guest, if you please."

More cygards descended. They tied both her wrists together with the rope and yanked her toward the front of the chamber, which was filled with elegantly clad people. Despite her efforts to free herself, her rope was fastened to a metal ring, adjacent to another prisoner—a young man with sandy hair and blue eyes. Kira's traveling cloak was yanked from her body, and as she gazed up into Mandral's face, she felt...nothing but the most passionate dislike she'd ever felt for another human being. Somehow, in a single moment, she'd slipped from his poisonous grasp. Her eyes riveted on the prisoner to her right. Could this mere boy be the reason for her deliverance?

Impossible.

Filthy, with his hair sticking up every which way, the young fellow looked nothing like her ideal man. He wasn't even a warrior that she could tell, although his torn shirt revealed some burgeoning musculature. Then she noticed the boy's clan ring and transporter cuff. Was he the wizard who'd captivated Dorsit's imagination? Well, no matter the reason for her sudden cure, it had come too late for them both. With no weapons and tied up like horn-snouted wild porcinians ready for the spit, they were at Mandral's mercy.

A NOTE FROM THE AUTHOR

In the Yden Trilogy, I introduce Quixoran of the Dragon Clan, Jon Hansen's wizard grandfather. Although Jon's grandmother Elina is mentioned in the tale, she has died by the time Jon finds his way to Dragon Isle.

Just for fun, I wrote a short story about Quixoran when he's about Jon's age. He went by the nickname Ran back then, and the story is about how he meets his future wife, Elina of the Moons Clan. As Shakespeare wrote, however, "the course of true love never did run smooth." In "Ran," several characters are introduced who show up later in the Yden series.

"The Temporary Wizard of Locklynn" is based on a short story originally appearing in Aurora Wolf Magazine and in the Aurora of the Mists Anthology. Ilene McMillan and her brother Ian are characters introduced in *Secrets of Yden* (Book Two of the Yden Series). "The Temporary Wizard of Locklynn" takes place several years after the end of the Yden trilogy.

Enjoy!

Suzanne G. Rogers

RAN

AN YDEN SHORT STORY

GREAT IDEA

CHAPTER ONE

$\mathcal{B}$ecause he was itching to make progress on his latest creation, Ran of the Dragon Clan wriggled out of wizard training for the morning. He transported to his outdoor art studio, in a grassy clearing next to a gurgling waterfall. With a pleasant summer breeze caressing his long blond hair, the young apprentice picked up a chisel and mallet and resumed work on a green-tinted soapstone carving of a water nymph. Just as he made a critical cut, Dell of the Unicorn Clan materialized nearby.

With the sudden interruption, Ran flinched and his chisel went astray. *"Newtics!"*

Dell took his friend literally. Puzzled, he searched for rodents in the grass. "I don't see any newtics, Ran." When he noticed the nymph's ear had been severed, he winced. "Oops."

While Ran used a repair spell to put his mistake to rights, Dell admired the sculpture. The luminous stone nymph was seemingly alive.

"I admit your work is extraordinary, but why carve the rock with tools when you can use magic? It takes so long to do it by hand."

"That's the whole point, Dell. I enjoy the process of creating beauty. Wizards can be too impatient."

"Speaking of which—"

"The answer is *no*. I already told you, I'm not interested."

"You have to get out and socialize."

"I don't have to do anything."

"Just because you completely choked when you met my cousin Marin, doesn't mean it'll happen every time."

"I didn't choke. Who said I choked?"

"Marin."

Embarrassed, Ran studied a nick in his chisel.

"This whole girl thing takes practice," Dell said. "You need to go places where you can meet them. It's the only way you'll ever have a female companion who's not made from stone."

The young Dragon Clan wizard shot his friend a level look. "Surely you didn't transport here to insult me."

"Um, well, no. Actually, I had a really great idea."

Ran folded his arms across his broad chest. "Oh? Your last really great idea got us both into trouble."

"Never mind that. All the other apprentices will be traveling to the festival using their transporter cuffs, right? Well, I want to make an entrance."

"No one's stopping you."

"If we take Zyzzyx, people will notice us. It's not every wizard who flies on a dragon. Come on, Ran, it'll be fun. It's a harvest festival and there'll be all sorts of food booths."

"Food, huh?"

"Lots of food. Think about it...freshly roasted puleden, cinnamon battercakes, and lemon ices. Even Ubbliton cider."

Ran's stomach gurgled. "Are you buying?"

"Sure. There's a tournament for apprentices. I'll have a bag of gold when I win."

"Guess I'll bring my own money, then."

"You don't think I'll be victorious? You've got no faith in me."

"I've got plenty of faith, but the competition at those tournaments is steep and there's always a lot of cheating going on."

"We'll see about that. So does that mean you'll go?"

"You had me at battercakes."

SLEEPY-EYED, Ran stumbled from the house the next morning, just as Solegra had just peeked over the horizon. With a flash and a sound like a soft thunderclap, Dell transported nearby. The unicorn clan wizard's mouth cracked open in yawn so wide it seemed as if his head would split with the effort. Ran eyed his friend's splendid white robes, embroidered in silvery threads.

"Rather fancy clothes for a harvest festival, aren't they?"

"Not everybody is as tall and muscle-bound as you are. I need something to draw in the ladies. Besides which, haven't you heard that robes make the wizard?"

Ran glanced down at his own fawn-colored breeches, open broadcloth shirt, and knee-length boots. "Funny, I always thought it was my clan ring that made me a wizard."

After the two friends hiked to the adjacent open field, Ran whistled for his dragon. Zyzzyx appeared several minutes later, his bronze wings glowing in the sunrise. The beautiful creature spiraled downward and landed with a mighty thump. The backdraft from his wings flattened the surrounding grass and made Dell's robes flap.

Ran vaulted onto the huge dragon bareback, but Dell balked.

"Er…don't you have a saddle for those wizards who've never ridden a dragon before?"

"Zyzzyx wouldn't like it, and you don't want to make him mad." Ran grinned. "This was your idea, wasn't it?"

Dell gritted his teeth, braced his boot on the dragon's bent forearm, and settled himself behind Ran.

"Grip Zyzzyx firmly with your knees, and grab one of his spines," Ran said over his shoulder. "You'll be fine."

"Says you."

Ran bent down to pat his dragon on the neck. "Be gentle, my friend. We have a nervous guest."

Zyzzyx might ordinarily be expected to leap skyward on takeoff, but because of Ran's admonition, he trotted a few steps with his wings spread and lifted into the air like a leaf in the breeze. Nevertheless, as they gained altitude, a strangled moan found its way from Dell's throat.

"All right back there?" Ran asked.

Dell's voice was high-pitched. "I suppose."

Several minutes later, however, he seemed to settle in.

"This isn't so bad so long as I don't look down. It's a little relaxing, actually."

"Zyzzyx has never let me fall," Ran said.

"*Yet.* There's always a yet in there somewhere."

An hour later, Zyzzyx flew over the farm where the harvest festival was being held. Elyas of the Moons Clan had an extensive property, with acres of blue fruit trees and silver grapevines. Herds of puledens grazed in the fields below, scattering like newtics as the dragon's shadow crossed their paths.

"No hunting here, Zyzzyx," Ran murmured.

The dragon snorted his displeasure.

Dell slapped Ran's back to draw his attention to a large gathering below. "There it is. Make sure everyone sees us."

Zyzzyx dipped down toward the festival grounds, where an amphitheater had been conjured to host the tournament. Numerous booths formed a marketplace, where food and trinkets could be purchased. Elyas' house and stables were located within walking distance, as was a barn and pens for his animals.

To Dell's delight, people on the ground stopped to point and stare as they circled overhead. Unfortunately, a pen full of wooly goats panicked at the sight of the dragon. One of the creatures jumped a fence and ran amuck through the crowd.

"Uh-oh," Dell muttered.

"Is this the kind of entrance you had in mind?"

"Not so much."

PUFFERY

CHAPTER TWO

Ran landed Zyzzyx next to a cornfield, nearly dislodging Dell in the process. Both boys slid to the ground, and Ran gave his dragon a grateful pat on the neck.

"Thanks for the ride, Zyzzyx. Dell and I are both wearing our transporter cuffs, so we'll get home by ourselves."

With a trumpeting cry, the dragon leaped into the air and streaked off. As Ran watched Zyzzyx soar off, his chest filled with pride.

"How *dare* you fly that dragon here!"

Startled, Ran turned to see a girl pointing at him, her rosebud mouth pursed in anger. He stumbled backwards and nearly lost his balance.

"This is a *farm*, you horn-snouted porcinian! You've scared the animals half to death!"

"Uh…I…"

To his horror, he felt a dull flush creep across his face and his tongue seemed to be stuck to the roof of his mouth. Despite the flash of anger in her eyes, the girl was the most exquisite creature he'd ever seen. He should have just apologized, but at the

153

moment he was unable to articulate a sentence. Even worse, Dell was convulsing in silent laughter at his discomfort.

"Haven't you anything to say for yourself?" she demanded.

In truth, Ran couldn't think of a good defense, so he retreated into the lofty arrogance his elder brothers had always found infuriating. He strode over to his friend with a cocky swagger in his step. "Dell, this girl—"

"Elina," she supplied.

"*Elina* accuses me of being a porcinian. How shall I respond?"

Dell smothered a snicker. "Deny it."

"I certainly *do* deny it. I'm not a porcinian. Everyone knows that porcinians don't fly on dragons."

Ran grabbed Dell's arm and the two of them escaped by darting into the thicket of booths comprising the marketplace. They didn't stop running until they'd reached the far side.

"You told *her*," Dell chortled.

"Who was that?"

"Elina of the Moons Clan, I think. She's really pretty. Too bad she's mad at you."

"Thanks for that, Dell," Ran retorted. "You talked me into coming today to meet girls, not make them hate me."

"Hey, it's not my fault you got all high and mighty! All you needed to do was to apologize."

A sigh. "I know, but she caught me off guard."

Dell cocked a thumb toward the tournament registration table. "Come on, I need to enter the tournament before there's a long line."

Ran accompanied his friend to the table, where the attending wizard took Dell's entrance fee and affixed a number to the back of his robe. As the Unicorn Clan wizard signed his name on the scroll of duelists, the attendant gave Ran an appraising look.

"How about you, young wizard? Care to test your magical mettle?"

"No, thanks. I live in a house full of older brothers who test my mettle daily. My mettle has been fully certified."

"Suit yourself."

Ran's clan ring began to sting his finger, announcing the arrival of a hostile wizard. He glanced up to see Homa of the Shark Clan approach, flanked by his close friend, Fozt.

"If it isn't Ran." Homa made the name sound like a sneer, and Fozt snickered.

"My friends call me Ran, but you can call me Quixoran. Actually, I'd rather you not call me anything."

"I see you're not entering the tournament." Homa exchanged an amused glance with Fozt. "Afraid of losing?"

"Not at all. Unlike you, Homa, I've nothing to prove."

Ran and Dell brushed past the two young wizards and waded into the marketplace.

"Homa doesn't mix well with people." Ran rubbed his finger, which was still stinging from his clan ring's alarm.

His friend was also flexing his hand. "Because of him, my clan ring sent a warning straight up my arm. Why does he come out in public?"

"I don't know, but he's really persistent at it."

Dell glanced back at the table, where Homa was signing the registration scroll. "Gah! He's entering the tournament!"

"Don't worry, you can take him."

"I don't know. Like you said, there's always cheating going on, and he's the biggest cheat around."

"I'll watch him for you. If he tries anything, I'll turn him into stone." Ran breathed in the heady food aromas wafting in their direction. "These smells are making me hungry!"

"Me too. If I don't get something to eat, I may just go back and punch Homa in the face."

"We can't have that. If you start punching him, the rest of us will get envious and have to join in."

After they bought bowls of steamed grain, skewers of roasted meat, and a couple of tankards of Ubbliton cider, they sat underneath a shady tree to eat. A few minutes later, Nedd of the Bee Clan joined them. Although he was the same age as Ran and Dell, his short stature and baby face made him appear younger.

"Hello! Have you met Elina of the Moons Clans yet? She's so sweet."

"I've heard she has a temper." Dell waggled his eyebrows at Ran.

"Really? I've never heard her say a cross word to anyone," Nedd said. "Who told you that?"

"Ask Ran."

"I wouldn't know." Ran shot Dell a withering glance. "Unfortunately, Elina and I haven't been properly introduced."

Homa drifted past. "Hey, Nedd, do you want me to conjure a milking stool for you to stand on?"

The Bee Clan wizard rolled his eyes. "Oh, a *short* joke. I've never heard one before, or one quite so witty."

"Never mind, Nedd. Homa's a witless wizard," Dell said.

"Hey, Homa, Nedd may be compact, but he's got ten times your ability," Ran called out. "I'll bet that bit of reality stings."

As the scowling Shark Clan wizard skulked off, a crooked smile crept onto Nedd's lips.

"Thanks, Ran. Do you really believe I'm better than Homa?"

"Absolutely." His reply, although heartfelt, was more from loyalty than true conviction.

"In that case, your next tankard of cider is on me," Nedd said.

"Hey, I believe it too!" Dell exclaimed. "You're way, way more talented."

"Three ciders, then." The Bee Clan wizard rose. "You know

what? I wasn't going to enter the tournament, but you've given me confidence. I'm going to sign up."

After he strode off toward the registration table, Ran gave Dell an alarmed glance. "Oh, no! He's going to be slaughtered, and it's all our fault!"

"Yes, but you started it! What'd you have to go puff him up for?"

"I just felt sorry for him." Ran groaned. "Could this day get any worse?"

"Don't ask."

TOURNAMENT

CHAPTER THREE

They finished their meal just as Nedd returned with a number on his robe and three tankards of ale in his hands. After Ran and Dell took one apiece, a repulsion spell sent Nedd's tankard spilling down the front of his robes. A few yards away, Homa sputtered with unconcealed glee.

Nedd turned pink with anger. "Did either of you see who did that?"

"I think we all know who did it," Ran muttered.

"Homa's always throwing his weight around," Ned said. "I wish someone would put that shark in his place."

The Bee Clan wizard murmured a cleaning spell to remove the yellow stains, and Homa's resulting mocking laughter made Ran's temper flare. He thrust his tankard into Dell's hand.

"Hold this for me. I'll be right back."

He strode toward the tournament entrance table, paid the entrance fee, and inked his name at the bottom of the scroll of duelists. The attending wizard fastened a number to Ran's shirt with a sticking spell.

"Spirit of the competition finally got to you, eh, young fellow?"

"Something like that."

As Ran rejoined his friends, Dell frowned and smacked him on the arm.

"Why'd you have to enter the tournament? There's no way I can win now!"

"What? You've been prodding me to enter a tournament for eons!"

"Yes, but I never thought you *would.*"

Nedd snorted with laughter.

The Shark Clan wizard's voice was raised in a taunt. "Now that the Dragon Clan wizard is in the tournament, we should all go home."

"You might as well quit right now, Homa," Ran replied. "The last wizard standing today won't be you."

"Won't be you either."

Homa formed an everlasting orb with his hands and hurled it at Ran. It missed, but Ran retaliated by retrieving the orb and slinging it back at him. Homa ducked, unfortunately, and the orb smacked the hind end of a newly shorn yama. The winged yama squealed and took flight, heading toward a nearby batter-cake booth. Ran, Nedd, and Dell tried to head the yama off, but it took the help of several security wizards to get the frightened animal under control. To Ran's complete dismay, Elina arrived just in time to hear the head security wizard give him a lecture on dueling outside the tournament amphitheater.

Her cool glance seemed to lance right through him.

"Causing problems again? Is that common with Dragon Clan wizards or is it a personal issue?"

Although he opened his mouth to make a clever rejoinder, he couldn't think of one. She sauntered off, leaving him feeling clumsy and stupid. Ran didn't have long to suffer, however, because the tournament was starting, and his number was up first. As he rolled up his sleeves and reported to the arena, a sudden apprehension tightened his gut. If Elina was in the stadium, the tournament stakes had just grown exponentially. He couldn't afford to lose in front of her.

As the tournament progressed, Ran, Dell, and Nedd managed to win their initial matches to progress to the semi-finals. Unfortunately, so did Homa and Fozt. To Dell's dismay, he was ultimately defeated by a Leopard Clan wizard and had to content himself with coaching Ran.

"You're unbeatable with that stone trick of yours."

"Maybe."

"You sound worried."

"Well…now that everyone's seen it, some wizard might have had time to devise a countermeasure."

"Your brothers have never figured out a way around it."

A chuckle. "No, they haven't, which is why they always attack me from behind." He scanned the amphitheater stands.

"Who are you looking for?"

"No one in particular."

"She's not here."

"I don't know who you mean."

Dell flicked his eyes skyward. "Elina, of course. She's staffing a healer tent just outside the amphitheater." He gestured toward the bandage on his hand. "She put some ointment on a cut I got in my first match."

Mixed emotions followed the news. Although Elina's absence at the tournament made Ran feel less self-conscious, he might end up the victor. If she wasn't here to witness his triumph, how else would he hope to win her over? As he remembered her frosty gaze, however, he suddenly realized he had no chance of impressing the girl whatsoever. He ought to focus on teaching Homa a lesson, and forget about Elina. If he could beat Fozt, the Shark Clan wizard would be next.

That, at least, was a match he would savor with great anticipation.

While Ran was preparing for his duel with Fozt, the Turtle Clan wizard seemed to be arguing with Homa on the far side of the arena. Ran tugged on Dell's arm and pointed.

"Wonder what that's all about? Looks like Fozt is really angry with Homa."

"Maybe he finally noticed Homa's stench?" Dell suggested.

"Better late than never. I've never liked Fozt much, but he could do better than to associate himself with Homa."

A few moments later, the next match was announced. Ran and Fozt met in the center of the field and clasped their wrists under the watchful supervision of the referee wizard.

"Good luck, Fozt," Ran said.

Fozt wouldn't meet his eyes. "Yeah."

When the match began, Fozt fired a burst of repulsion spells that Ran parried without much effort. When Ran went on offense, however, the Turtle Clan wizard had a formidable shield spell he could not penetrate. He encircled Fozt with a dust funnel, hoping to spot a chink in his armor, but none presented itself. Flummoxed, Ran took a defensive posture with his own shield spell and waited for his opponent's attack.

To his shock, the assault came as a blast of sound; a deep boom that lifted him off his feet and sent him flying. His shield spell was ineffective against such an attack, and as he laid flat, his ears buzzed, and his nerves were jangled. Although he was disoriented, he knew he was about to lose the match. Still sprawled in the dirt, he formed the largest everlasting orb he'd ever conjured, hoping it would temporarily blind his opponent. The light was so bright, onlookers threw their arms up over their faces to shield their eyes. His ears were still buzzing, but his ploy gave him a few moments to collect his wits. With his palms touching the ground, Ran sent a tremor into the ground to knock Fozt off his feet. He extinguished the everlasting orb and before Fozt's eyes could adjust, he turned him into stone.

His victory over the Turtle Clan wizard had been surprisingly difficult, Ran acknowledged. Fozt was a quiet wizard whose only distinguishing characteristic up until now was associating himself with Homa. Most apprentices lacked the sort of power he'd just demonstrated, and he'd earned Ran's grudging respect. After the referee pronounced him the winner, Ran reversed his spell and Fozt returned to flesh and blood. Ran crossed over to him and extended a sportsmanship-like hand.

"Good match, Fozt."

"Yeah. Sorry."

"What?"

Fozt blasted Ran with a strong wave of repulsion. Completely unprepared, Ran was sent flying into the wall of the arena, hit his head, and blacked out.

CHAPTER FOUR

Ran came to consciousness with something cool and moist on his face. He opened his eyes to discover he was lying on a cot with a cold cloth draped over his forehead and an angel hovering nearby. Alarmed, he bolted upright, and his vision swam. With a moan, he dropped his aching head in his hands.

"Lie still. You took quite a bad blow."

The angel's voice sounded soothing...and uncomfortably familiar. If he was injured, that meant he was in Elina's healer tent. Ran forced one eye open to get a better look at her. She had gray-green eyes the color of a stormy sea, and her hair formed a strawberry-blond halo around her face. Her skin was so smooth it resembled an alabaster carving. At the moment, her expression was one of concern and sympathy.

"How long have I been out?" His voice sounded raspy.

"Your friends carried you in here twenty minutes ago. The tournament is almost over."

Panic gave him a jolt. "I have to beat Homa in the final!" Despite the pain in his head, he swung his feet to the ground.

"You can't move, Ran. You must forfeit."

"Not going to happen. Homa put Fozt up to hurting me. He cheated and I can't let him win." He tried to stand, without much success.

Elina made a frustrated noise deep in her throat. "I can see nothing will deter you. Just wait a moment. I have something which will improve your condition."

After she dabbed an ointment on his forehead and temples, his headache diminished, and his vision stopped going double. As far as Ran was concerned, she really was an angel.

"Thank you, Elina," he said. "I'm sorry about what happened earlier with the dragon. I really didn't mean to cause trouble."

Elina raised an eyebrow. "I suspect you're the very essence of trouble, Quixoran of the Dragon Clan."

"You know my name?"

"I make it my business to know the names of all the worst troublemaking wizards." Despite her words, she gave him a glance from underneath her lashes. "Besides which, the dragon gave it away."

"Call me Ran." He extended his hand. "Will you help me walk? I'm still dizzy."

It was true enough, but as he gazed at Elina, he couldn't tell if it was his head or his heart that was spinning. When her hand grasped his, he felt a delicious shiver dance across his skin. Once he was on his feet, she let go. He deliberately swayed toward her and was rewarded with her arm around his waist. She glanced up, catching him with a pleased grin on his lips.

"Oh, you!" She stepped back. "Like I said before, you're trouble."

"The good kind, I hope."

"That remains to be seen."

She accompanied him from the tent, but as they approached the arena, a huge roar told them that the final match had just concluded.

A wave of disappointment hit Ran and his shoulders slumped. "Oh, no. I'm too late."

Crowds had emptied the stands and were filling the field when they entered, so he couldn't see the winner at first. Although he braced himself before glancing at the final score-board, he was still shocked to read the name of the winner.

"What? It can't be!"

"Look!" Elina pointed.

Nedd was hoisting the winner's purse of gold aloft for all to see. When he met Ran's gaze, he gave him a beaming smile. Delighted laughter bubbled up from Ran's core and he shouted his congratulations. The Bee Clan wizard's victory, although unexpected, was almost sweeter than his own would have been.

Homa had skulked off to one side. His nose was red and swollen and he wore a sour expression. Ran excused himself so he could speak to the Shark Clan wizard in private.

"You're a bully and a cheat, Homa. I'm glad you got what you deserved."

"And you're a self-righteous, arrogant bore!"

To Ran's astonishment, Homa landed a sucker punch to his jaw. He staggered back a few paces and rubbed the injury. "I'm so glad you hit me."

"Why?"

"Because I get to retaliate."

With a flick of his fingers, Ran turned the Shark Clan wizard to stone from the feet up. To his amusement, the crowds swirled around the newly created statue, unconcerned. He spotted an ebullient Dell several yards away and hastened over to grab his arm.

"Hey, I missed the action. How did Nedd win?"

"You should've seen it, Ran," Dell chortled. "Homa jumped from one flashy attack to another and made a complete idiot of himself."

"No surprise there."

"It came kind of close a couple of times, but Nedd parried each of Homa's moves. Then BAM, he took Homa out with a swarm of magical bees. Homa ran around in circles and screamed like a little girl. It was *great!*"

For the second time that day, Ran was impressed. "Nedd conjured *bees?* I didn't know he could do that. What happened to Fozt?"

"Sent home in disgrace."

"Homa put him up to it, you know."

"I figured as much, but Fozt wasn't talking." Dell's smile slipped a little. "I'm sorry about what happened. If it wasn't for Fozt, I'm pretty sure you'd have won."

"It doesn't matter." Ran glanced toward Elina, who was talking to her father a short distance away. It had taken a blow to the head to finally loosen Ran's tongue. "As it turned out, everything worked out for the best."

Nedd bounded over. After his triumphant win, he looked taller somehow.

Ran pounded him on the back. "You did it, Nedd! I'm really happy for you, but I wish I could've watched the final match in person."

"I wouldn't have had the confidence to win if it hadn't been for you, Ran. You and Dell stuck up for me earlier, and when I saw what happened with Fozt, I knew I had to beat Homa for all of us."

Dell grinned. "What are friends for?"

"Hey, how about a tankard of Ubbliton cider?" Ran asked. "I'm buying."

As TWILIGHT DESCENDED, the harvest festival drew to a close. Wizards and their families had begun to transport home, but

Dell and Ran lounged next to the cider booth, enjoying a final tankard of the delicious beverage.

"So Elina's not mad at you anymore?" Dell asked. "Too bad you don't have an excuse to see her anytime soon."

"Don't be so sure I don't. I spoke with her father after the tournament, and he agreed to let me carve her likeness, by hand."

Dell's eyebrows rose. "Which, I've been told, takes a great deal of patience?"

"And many weeks of sittings."

"Say, do you think you could teach me to carve? Nedd's sister is really cute."

"Get your own ploy, Dell."

Elina approached, her eyes snapping with anger.

"Uh, oh. What did you do now?" Dell murmured.

"I've no idea."

She stopped in front of Ran with her arms akimbo. "Are you planning to leave Homa as a statue? He's been that way for hours!"

He shrugged. "He looks so much better in stone."

"The Festival is over, Ran. Lift your spell."

"Has anyone ever mentioned you're a little bossy?"

Her gray-green eyes narrowed. "Do you have a problem with a woman who knows her own mind?"

"Definitely. Perhaps you can help me with that?"

Although she made a sound of disgust, her lips curved in a smile. Ran's heart melted.

"Now you've done it," he said.

"Done what?"

"That smile of yours has convinced me to show mercy toward ugly statues. I think you're beginning to be a good influence on me."

Ran waved his fingers toward the amphitheater. Moments later, Homa's howl of rage reached their ears.

Dell stuck his elbow in Ran's ribs. "We should probably depart before the shark bites."

"Until we meet again, Elina." Ran gave her a wink.

The End

THE TEMPORARY WIZARD OF LOCKLYNN

AN YDEN SHORT STORY

A REAL WIZARD

CHAPTER ONE

The mayor of Locklynn gave Ilene McMillan a quizzical glance. "But you're female. You can't be a wizard."

Ilene sighed inwardly. She'd heard the same thing at the last six villages she'd visited. The people of Yden really were behind the times, but she had to be polite nevertheless.

"I most certainly *am* an Eagle Clan wizard." She flashed the mayor a winning smile as she showed him her Clan ring. "In fact, I was trained by Quixoran."

"The Dragon Clan wizard himself, huh?" Mayor Henryr's eyebrows lifted for a moment before drawing together in a frown. "Well, even so, it doesn't matter. We've already got a wizard working for us and we don't need any more help."

"No?"

From Ilene's vantage point in the center of Locklynn, she surveyed the town. The dirt surface of the main road was marred with ruts and indentations, many of the hand-carved rooftop shingles on the quaint shops were either loose or missing, and more than a few leaded-glass windowpanes were cracked. A short distance away, a desperate farmer labored to pump water into a long wooden trough for his waiting flock of wooly goats. Despite the man's best efforts, the spigot produced only a thin trickle for the thirsty, bleating animals. Overall, Ilene was unimpressed. Locklynn had undoubtedly been charming in the past, but it was shabby and rundown at present.

"Begging your pardon, Mayor, but your wizard seems to be as useful as a leaky teapot."

The mayor bristled. "Poor Kipp's been melancholy since his wife died."

"I'm very sorry for his loss, but that's not going to replenish the water in your wells or repair your roads." Ilene sighed as she picked up the knapsack at her feet. "I'll fix that pump for you, and then I'll be off. Thank you for your time, and I hope your wizard gets back to work soon."

As she stepped off the wooden boardwalk into the street, Ilene tried not to let her shoulders slump. Although she was reluctant to admit it, Locklynn's wizard wasn't the only one fighting off a bout of melancholy. After several years of intensive study with the most illustrious wizard on Yden, Ilene and her twin brother Ian had finally become full-fledged wizards. About a month ago, her brother had secured a position in a nice little mountainside hamlet called Spriteburg, but things had not gone so smoothly for Ilene. Everywhere she went, she'd run into resistance. People weren't comfortable with the fact she was female, and had no problem saying so. When Quixoran of the Dragon Clan had agreed to train female apprentices, he'd bucked a longstanding, males-only tradition on Yden. Ilene had been amongst the first class of newly minted female wizards, and was eager to prove herself. Unfortunately, she'd underestimated the challenges of securing a job.

Ilene skirted several puddles of mud left from recent early spring showers. Rainwater had pooled in the craters of the neglected thoroughfare, making it hazardous to wagon wheels, horses, and ankles alike. Had it been up to her, she would have magically smoothed the dirt surface and covered it with something attractive and picturesque, like cobblestones or bricks. Fresh from her apprenticeship, she was brimming with exciting ideas and limitless energy. All she needed was a chance to show what she could do.

The farmer glanced up from the pump as she approached, exasperation etched on his sweat-streaked, craggy face. "I'm sorry, lass, but the well is running dry. You'll have to drink from the one on the far side of town."

A striking blonde had emerged from the nearby Spinning Wheel Tavern, with a bucket in hand. She arrived at the pump in time to overhear the farmer's words.

"That's largely thanks to you, Natty Wilkins!" She drove her point home with an index finger. "If you didn't water your wooly goats in town every other day, the well wouldn't have run dry so quickly."

The farmer winced. "Oh come now, Gert. My goats become thirsty, just like any other creatures."

"There's a stream on your property," the woman shot back. "Do us all a favor and water them there."

"My stream is nearly down to a memory." Natty shook his head. "Even with the recent rain."

Ilene cleared her throat. "If you'll both stand clear, I'll fix the well."

Natty made a sound of disbelief. "A young girl like you?"

She brushed aside his condescension. "It's an easy spell to manage."

Although Ilene raised her Clan ring hand to perform the magic, the sun-wizened farmer shielded the pump with his broad frame.

"Best let a real wizard do that, lass."

A tight smile masked Ilene's annoyance. "I *am* a real wizard, I assure you. Now please step aside before fresh spring water begins accidentally running from your nose."

The farmer refused to budge. "I don't know what you're playing at, but leave off before you do real damage. The last thing we need around here is a plague of toads or some such mischief from magic gone awry."

"Natty, did you ever meet an insult you didn't like?" Gert turned to Ilene. "Never mind him; he's been raising wooly goats so long he's got wool between his ears. I'd heard Quixoran of the Dragon Clan was training female wizards. It's high time, in my opinion, but I never thought I'd come across one in Locklynn."

"I was hoping to settle in a small town." Ilene glanced back at the mayor, who was chatting with one of the town's residents outside his office. "But it seems there's a wizard working here already."

"I suppose that depends on your definition of working." Gert grabbed the farmer by the arm and hauled him to one side. "Let her fix the well, Natty, unless you want to be banned from my tavern for life."

"Now, Gert!"

"I mean it, old man." She gave the farmer a level glance. "No more cold ale for you, no matter how hard you beg."

The farmer's expression was dour, but he shuffled off behind one of his goats. In short order, Ilene enchanted the pump to produce a steady, clean flow. Natty stuck his hand under the water and brought his moistened fingers to his tongue.

"Well, I'll be a toad's behind." He chortled in amazement. "It's perfect!"

"'Course it is, and you *are* a toad's behind." Gert held her empty bucket under the pump. "This lady is a real wizard."

After the bucket was full, the woman nodded her thanks and returned to the tavern. Ilene continued to fill the trough with clear, cool sparkling water for the goats or any other parched creatures that happened to pass by. The animals nudged Ilene out of the way as they clustered around the trough to drink.

"Er...forgive me, Wizard." Natty touched the brim of his hat. "I guess I spoke out of turn."

"No offense taken, but I hope you'll give the next female wizard you meet a chance. At present, only a handful of wizards on Yden are women, but eventually they will become commonplace. If you'll excuse me, I'll be on my way."

She turned to leave.

"Wait!" Mayor Henryr bounded over to gape at Ilene's handiwork. "Perhaps I was too hasty, Eagle Clan Wizard. I can't make any long-term promises, but there may be a few chores in Locklynn you could address...until Kipp's back at it."

Relief lifted the weight on Ilene's shoulders and brought a smile to her face. Although a temporary job was hardly guaranteed employment, it was the best and only offer she'd had.

CRY ME A RIVER

CHAPTER TWO

Ilene accompanied Mayor Henryr into the rustic Spinning Wheel Tavern, where they discussed the town's priorities over a welcome midday meal. The lamp-lit tavern was so dark inside that Ilene was obliged to fashion a small everlasting orb in order to see her chicken potpie properly. She hoisted the shining sphere upward until it came to rest underneath one of the heavy wooden beams overhead.

"I daresay my wife would enjoy an everlasting orb at our house." The mayor gaped at the orb, clearly impressed. "It's difficult for her to knit by lamplight after both suns have set."

Mayor Henryr bent to scribble the task at the top of what was proving to be a lengthy list. Ilene's spirits rose; her stay in Locklynn seemed assured—at least for the near term. At minimum, she'd be able to count on the mayor as a reference. If the town's wizard remained absent, perhaps the job would continue indefinitely.

After the lunch crowd thinned out, the mayor beckoned to the blonde. "Gert, this is Ilene of the Eagle Clan. Ilene, Gert is the owner of this fine establishment."

"We've met." The young woman gave Ilene a broad smile. "I'm glad you didn't let Natty chase you off with his bad manners. The old farmer bleats a lot, but he's harmless."

Ilene smiled. "A bit of convincing is all he needed."

"Do you have a room for our temporary wizard?" Mayor Henryr asked. "The town of Locklynn will pay the rent."

"Aye." Gert nodded. "But instead of payment in gold, I've got a great many tasks that need doing around here. I'd even throw in meals."

"Done." Ilene gestured to her empty plate. "I've never had better chicken potpie."

"Good." The mayor rubbed his hands together. "I'll let you settle in today, Ilene, but I've got a mountain of work for you bright and early tomorrow morning."

"I'll be ready."

After Mayor Henryr left with his list, Gert showed Ilene up a flight of stairs to the floor situated over the tavern. The first door on the left opened to a tiny room containing only a single bed and a chest of drawers.

Gert's expression was apologetic. "I'm sorry it's so small, but it's the only spare room I have."

The space was clean, but so cozy the bed was wedged underneath the steeply sloping roof. Nevertheless, a great deal of natural light flooded in from the bay window, which had a view of the town square.

Ilene dropped her knapsack on the bed and gave her new landlady a smile. "I like it."

"I'm glad. Don't sit up in the middle of the night or you'll hit your head." Gert frowned at Ilene's knapsack. "Is that the only bag you have?"

"Actually, it holds a lot more than you'd think. There's an enlargement spell on the inside."

"I'll take your word for it." Gert peered at the bag suspiciously, as if it were about to explode. "I don't mind admitting magic sometimes makes my head whirl, but I can't wait to see more."

"Now that you mention it, do you mind if I make some minor adjustments in here?"

The young woman shrugged. "I suppose not, so long as your changes aren't permanent."

In the next moment, Ilene magically raised the roof several feet, and extended the walls until the room was far larger than before.

Gert gasped and took a half step back. "I thought you were just going to change the curtains!"

"Don't worry, nothing's visible from the street," Ilene said quickly. "If it's too much, I'll remove the enlargement spell."

"No, I'd rather you leave it this way forever!" The woman did a pirouette in the new space. "In fact, you can enlarge my room across the hall."

As Locklynn's temporary wizard, Ilene stayed busy working spells. Her magic ensured that the bread oven would always be the proper temperature for baking, and the casks of ale would remain icy cold even on the hottest days of summer. She magically cleaned and repaired the fabric cushions covering the benches and chairs, and changed their color from faded beige to an attractive clover green. To Gert's delight, she also enchanted the decorative spinning wheel in the corner with a perpetual motion spell. Just for fun, she added an illusion spell to make it appear as if the device were producing spun gold. In Ilene's opinion, the end product rather resembled her landlord's fair hair.

Gert shook her head in amazement as she admired the

display. "It never would have occurred to me to enchant a spinning wheel. I imagine once word gets out, folks will come in to the tavern just to watch it spin."

"And hopefully purchase a few tankards of ale at the same time."

"Exactly my thought."

The woman stepped behind the long varnished wood bar, filled two tankards with frothy beverages, and beckoned Ilene over to a stool.

"You've earned a break." Gert plunked a tankard in front of Ilene and raised hers in a toast. "With my compliments."

"Thank you." Ilene drank her ale, glad for the cold refreshment. "This is delicious." She scooped up a bit of the foam with a fingertip and turned it into tiny silver snowflakes with a puff of air from her lips. "And pretty, too."

Gert giggled. "Not only are you a competent wizard, but you're creative as well."

Ilene tucked a strand of her curly dark locks behind one ear. "Wizards are tasked with making life easier for people, but their methods don't have to be dull."

"Can you put a spell on my tavern to keep it full of customers?" Gert's smile slipped. "To be honest, Locklynn is withering away from neglect." She gestured toward the empty room. "I'm afraid my business is dying along with it."

"I'll do my absolute best to spruce up the town in the time I'm here." She took another sip of ale. "I can already see Locklynn's potential. In top form, it'll be a charming place for travelers to stop."

"I'm glad you've come." Even though they were alone in the room, Gert lowered her voice. "We all love Kipp of the Bear Clan, but he hasn't been around very much since he lost his wife."

"So I heard," Ilene said. "How long has it been?"

"Oh, I think we're coming up on three turns now."

Turns were roughly equivalent to years on Ilene's native Earth.

"The poor soul is still unable to work after all this time? He and his wife must have had a long and happy marriage."

"They were married less than a turn, but Kipp was inconsolable when Ferra left him."

"Left him?" Ilene was confused. "Mayor Henryr told me she died."

"Out of respect to Kipp, we all pretend that's what happened." Gert shrugged. "Ferra was a very attractive girl, you see, and she had ambitions that couldn't be satisfied in a small town like Locklynn. Kipp can't quite get over her."

"Can't he?" Ilene's sympathy for the Bear Clan wizard evaporated. "Forgive me for being so blunt, but Kipp sounds like a big baby."

Gert stifled a laugh. "You're right, of course, but he's *our* big baby." She paused. "I wish the right man would fall just as deeply in love with me some day."

Ilene wrinkled her nose. "In my case, I don't think such a man exists. I'll probably never marry."

"Why would you say a thing like that? You've created quite a stir in the short while you've been here. Several gentlemen asked me about you while you were dining with the mayor."

"First of all, I'd never consider falling in love with a man unless he were best friends with my twin brother, Ian. And secondly, it takes more than a comely face to pique my interest. If Kipp of the Bear Clan is still obsessed with Ferra, he must be daft in the head."

"I wouldn't be quite so hard on the man. In his defense, Ferra was extremely beautiful."

"So is the sunset!" Ilene made a sound of disgust. "Men are too concerned with beauty."

"True." Gert gave her a sidelong glance. "Nevertheless, you'll want to remember that when you meet Kipp."

"Why?"

"He's the most handsome man I've ever seen."

"Humpf!" Ilene raised her tankard. "Without the proper character, good looks count for very little."

THE WOOLIHOPPERS

CHAPTER THREE

Mayor Henryr's chores seemed to multiply like the musical springtime wildflowers sprouting up in the fields, but Ilene dove into the work with relish. Locklynn's residents had accumulated a pent up demand for a wizard's services, and it seemed as if she'd arrived just in time. Her stay lengthened into weeks—long enough for her to discover she'd stumbled into a unique and whimsical place. The town's picturesque stone cottages, winding streams, and verdant countryside reminded her of Scotland, where she'd been born.

Locklynn was originally founded on textiles, she learned, and a great many of the region's farms raised wool-producing creatures called yamas. The horned and winged animals resembled a cross between sheep dogs and llamas—if llamas had small wings, of course. Ilene paid house calls to the outlying farms, where she was tasked with enchanting the sweet-tempered animals to produce different tints of wool. Afterward, the yamas tended to flock by hue. From a distance, the grassy fields appeared to be covered with moving streaks of color.

Yamas were shorn in late spring for their gloriously abundant wool, and the town always hosted a shearing festival in celebration. The resulting influx of visitors contributed greatly to Locklynn's fortunes, so the townspeople worked to make sure the upcoming festival would be a tremendous success. To that end, Ilene connected the mayor's office to the Wiznet magical mailbox system rapidly spreading across Yden, thereby allowing festival announcements to be sent out by the hundreds.

Ten days before the festival, the mayor pounced on Ilene as she left the tavern for work.

"We have a problem, Wizard." His expression was uncharacteristically sober. "An infestation of woolihoppers has settled at the Goery farm and they're eating the wool straight off his yamas."

"Woolihoppers? Are those some kind of insects?" Ilene asked, baffled.

"Yes, and they swarm most often after we've had an unusually dry winter." Mayor Henryr wrung his hands in a panic. "If we don't stop them, they'll eat through the town's whole crop of wool, and the festival will be ruined!"

She shook her head. "I don't know any magic specific to insect infestations, but Kipp should know what to do."

"He's holed up in his house and won't come out."

"What a galoot! Take me to the man and I'll see if I can pry the spell out of him."

Ilene and the mayor set off at a good clip. Just outside town, the mayor led her onto a weed-choked path through a swath of forest, and shortly thereafter to a slow-moving stream. When Ilene paused on the footbridge to admire the view, a fat laughing frog on the bank giggled, releasing a wave of toxic magic.

"Oh, no." Ilene exclaimed. "Watch out, Mayor!"

She easily blocked the wave, but it hit Mayor Henryr even as he ran to the far side of the bridge. He was obliged to put his hands on his knees, gasping for breath, until his lengthy fit of laughter passed.

Ilene was not amused. "A laughing frog is a nasty sort of creature to have guarding the bridge. I gather Kipp of the Bear Clan is unfriendly."

"He used to be as sunny as can be." The mayor wiped tears of mirth from his face with a large red handkerchief. "It was love gone wrong that changed him."

"If that's all it takes, we should all be warped," Ilene muttered.

As Mayor Henryr and Ilene drew closer to an underground dwelling built into the side of a hill, the wooden door and rounded windows suddenly faded away until they became a seamless part of the grass. In spite of her annoyance, Ilene was impressed.

"Not a bad illusion," she admitted. "You can't be bothered with visitors if they can't find your door."

"It's Kipp's way of telling us to leave," the mayor whispered.

"It is, is it?" Ilene cupped her hands around her mouth and aimed her voice at the hillside. "Come out and face me, you useless lump of a wizard."

Her taunt echoed off the trees, and Mayor Henryr recoiled. "I wouldn't address Kipp in that fashion! You could make him angry."

Ilene tossed her head as she moved forward. "That's exactly what I intend to do. Getting the man's dander up might snap him out of his melancholy. Don't you suppose he's been coddled long enough?"

Mayor Henryr made no reply. When she glanced back, she discovered the man had turned tail and was dashing across the footbridge as fast as his legs could carry him.

She sighed. "How like a politician to cut and run when things get difficult."

Undeterred, Ilene literally rolled up her sleeves, cast a reveal spell to locate Kipp's front door, and then pounded on the thick wood with the meaty part of her fist. "You're needed, you lazy lout! You'll have no peace from me until you show yourself."

When the door burst open, Ilene's first glimpse of the Bear Clan wizard was fearsome. Kipp was as thin as a bowl of gruel, his clothes were unkempt, and his wild reddish-brown mane had obviously avoided contact with a hairbrush for quite some time. The lower half of his face was covered in a bushy, ginger-colored beard, which served to draw attention to his unusual eyes. One was bright blue and the other was green, and both were flashing with anger. Despite his obvious hostility, however, Ilene's clan ring gave her no warning that the wizard was dangerous. Nevertheless, nothing would induce her to drop her guard.

"Get away from my door, woman," he thundered. "You've got the manners of a stray dog infested with pixienits."

"Speaking of infestations, while you've been sulking underground feeling sorry for yourself, the Goery farm has a nasty problem with woolihoppers," Ilene snapped. "If it's not too much bother, give me the spell and I'll deal with the pests."

"What are *you* going to do with a spell?"

Vestiges of her Scottish accent emerged. "I'm an Eagle Clan wizard, ye odd-eyed hermit."

"Ha! A slip of a girl like you is a wizard? You're joking."

Disrespect from a fellow wizard riled Ilene more than she'd anticipated. "Am I? Well then, let's both have a laugh."

Although she never laid a physical hand on him, Kipp suddenly flew through the air and landed in the stream nearby with a huge splash. She stood on the bank with her arms akimbo, glaring down at him.

"I'll thank ye not to underestimate a female wizard in the future. Enjoy yer bath. From the look of ye, doubtless you can use one."

Ilene used the magical transporter cuff on her wrist to transport herself directly to the Goery farm, where she'd worked the day prior. Unfortunately, she materialized into the center of pandemonium. Unhappy yamas were bleating in panic and flapping their wings as brown flying insects the size of a man's hand nibbled at their wool. She shuddered; the swarm was so thick that she couldn't take a step without treading on the distasteful insects. Poor Dane Goery and his family were shearing colorful fleeces as fast as they could in an attempt to save their crop from the jaws of the woolihoppers. Half the town had turned out to help, but it appeared to be a losing fight. As soon as the insects had been picked off a yama, more woolihoppers took their place.

Mayor Henryr rode up on horseback and dismounted. "Is Kipp coming?"

She shook her head. "I'm afraid we're on our own, but I'll do what I can."

Ilene jumped into the fray, using magic to draw off large numbers of woolihoppers and then freeze them. It was slow work, but for a while it seemed as if she was making headway. When another massive swarm of insects crested the horizon, however, there were gasps of dismay.

Dane Goery sank to his knees in defeat. "We're ruined."

STARTING OVER

CHAPTER FOUR

As the new swarm of woolihoppers blotted out the suns, Ilene's heart sank. Whatever she did now would be like using a garden hose to douse an inferno, but she refused to let the farmers give up hope.

"Keep shearing!"

She wiped the sweat from her eyes, gathered up her energy and prepared to face the incoming insects. As the swarm descended, however, Kipp finally materialized in a crackling flash of light. Although she was still angry with the wizard, her concern for the farmers overcame everything else.

"How can I help you?" she asked.

"Stay close. I'm going to protect the yamas, but I need you to continue killing woolihoppers."

When Kipp wove a spell over a herd of yamas that caused the grazing insects to whirr up overhead, Ilene magically blasted them with frigid air. The winged pests dropped to the grass like fat brown hail, making the ground appear as if it were covered with brown leaves.

"What does your spell do?" she asked.

"It makes the wool taste foul."

"Good one," she said. "I hadn't thought of that."

The two wizards moved across the herds of yamas, working together until the woolihopper menace was eliminated. Once the last insect was dead, Kipp magically swept the frozen creatures into a huge pile. Ilene vetoed his plan to burn the lot, and instead used a reduction spell until the pile resembled an anthill.

Kipp frowned. "I've not seen a reduction spell before."

His disrespect still stung. "If you stuck your head out of your den once in a while, you might learn a few things."

By the time she and Kipp returned to the farmhouse, Dane Goery had set up several casks of ale to reward his neighbors for coming to his aid. Kipp declined the cup offered to him, and waved off any expressions of gratitude.

"I'm just sorry for my late arrival. Excuse me, but I must transport to the other farms immediately to treat the yamas against any more woolihopper infestations."

The Bear Clan wizard vanished in a flash of light and sound like far-off thunder, leaving the scent of ozone in the air. As Ilene sipped her ale, she couldn't help remembering Gert's assertion that Kipp was the most handsome man she'd ever seen. Although Ilene freely acknowledged that Locklynn's wizard was powerful, she was baffled at the tavern keeper's observation. She could describe Kipp with many adjectives, but few would have been complimentary.

Mayor Henryr hastened over. "It appears that your approach with Kipp was better than ours. What did you say to him?"

Ilene laughed as she recalled the Bear Clan wizard sitting in the middle of the stream with a shocked expression on his face.

"You could say I threw a little cold water on the situation." She shrugged. "I hope for Locklynn's sake it does Kipp some long term good."

"I'll drink to that." The mayor hastened to get himself a cup of ale.

As Ilene scanned the jubilant faces of Dane Goery and his

friends, a surge of affection filled her up inside. Locklynn and its residents had grown on her over a very short period of time, and she was glad for their happiness. What a shame that the end of Kipp's hibernation meant the loss of a job and her new friends.

~

IN THE TAVERN'S common room after dinner that night, townspeople exchanged enthusiastic stories about their fierce battle against the woolihoppers. Ilene joined in from time to time, but she mostly enjoyed listening to the conversation. Her mood was becoming increasingly tinged with sadness at the realization she would be moving on very soon.

Gert slid into the chair next to her and gave her a worried smile. "Are you all right? Your green eyes look a little blue."

"I'll be fine, thank you. I imagine I should leave tomorrow so you can rent out my room for the festival."

The young woman cocked her head. "What? You and Locklynn are getting along famously, so why do you want to go?"

"I don't have a choice. I always knew my work here was temporary, and now that Kipp is back on duty, I must look for another job."

Gert's face fell. "It doesn't seem fair somehow."

Ilene forced a smile to her lips. "Perhaps once I'm settled into my next position, I'll come for a visit to see how you're getting along."

"Has Mayor Henryr told you that your services are no longer required?"

"N-No, but he doesn't have to spell it out."

"In that case, promise me you won't leave until after the festival. Kipp will probably have to ease back into his duties, and I'm sure there's plenty of work for you to do until then."

"Do you think so?" The steel band tightening across Ilene's

chest eased. "I'll stay, but only if you let me add extra guest rooms to the tavern. You can always use the extra accommodations even after the festival is over."

"You have a deal, even though I'm getting the better bargain."

OVER THE NEXT FEW DAYS, Ilene was too busy with festival preparations to contemplate her departure. Gert mentioned that Kipp was working out at the festival grounds, helping to erect a dance pavilion and food booths.

"It's so wonderful to see him out and about as a part of the community again," she said.

"That's great." Ilene forced herself to smile. "I'm glad the town is in such good hands."

At last, people began to pour into Locklynn in anticipation of the festivities. All the rooms at the Spinning Wheel Tavern were full, even the extra ones Ilene had magically created. In addition, most of Locklynn's residents allowed tourists to rent their spare bedrooms. Visitors also erected tents in the fields—so many, in fact, that the area resembled an enormous, sprawling campground. Shops were bursting with customers, and Ilene was glad she'd put so much effort into renewing the streets and buildings. For such a small town, Locklynn looked its best.

Her brother, Ian, arrived on the first day of the festival, bringing with him a large contingent of visitors from Spriteburg. The group included several merchants in search of yama fleeces and wool products. It was with a great deal of pride that Ilene watched Spriteburg merchants haggling over the vibrantly colored woolen lots in the open-air marketplace.

Ian nodded toward the vast display of woolen fleeces. "I recognize your excellent handiwork, Ilene. You've always had a fine eye for color."

"You're too kind." Her gaze fell to the lightweight cherry-red muffler around his neck. "What a beautiful scarf! Did you buy that from one of the booths?"

"Naw, I won it off a local gent in a game of cards at the campground this morning." He chuckled at the memory. "Poor fellow never knew what hit him."

Gert gave Ian a saucy wink as she strolled past. Ian's eyebrows rose and he glanced around to make sure her gesture was directed at him.

"Her name is Gert and she wants to meet you. Why don't you go introduce yourself?"

"I don't mind if I do." He straightened his clothes and combed his hair with his fingers. "How do I look?"

"As dazzling as ever." Ilene grabbed his arm before he could dart away. "Be sure to conduct yourself in a gentlemanly manner."

"I'm always a gentleman!"

"Ian, I'm perfectly serious." Ilene scowled. "Gert's not only my landlady, but she's a good friend."

Her brother's expression turned thoughtful. "I won't let ye down." He loped off in pursuit.

Moments later, another man sauntered over and gave her a nod. "Good afternoon."

"Good afternoon."

As Ilene stared at the man's profile, her mouth went dry. The stranger was young, clean-shaven and terribly handsome, with broad shoulders and a shock of thick red-brown hair.

"Er...welcome to Locklynn. You must be here for the festival?"

"I am. I have to say, the town looks much better than the last time I was here. Gert tells me you're the new wizard?"

"Aye," she replied, without thinking. "Well, actually, no. I'm just temporary."

"Maybe you should stick around." He chuckled. "I've heard the regular wizard is a useless lump and a lazy lout to boot."

"What?" When Ilene looked the man full in the face, she noticed the man had one green and one blue eye—both exceedingly mesmerizing. "I-I can't imagine where you heard that."

"I've no doubt it's true." He shrugged. "I also heard he's been sulking underground, feeling sorry for himself." The man shook his head. "Considering how he let the town languish, I expect he's rather ashamed of his behavior."

"I don't know Kipp at all, to be truthful." She bit her lip. "We didn't exactly meet under the best of circumstances."

"Perhaps you two could start over." He smiled. "If you're willing."

"Maybe so, but it won't be easy." She pointed to Ian, who'd cornered Gert next to a booth selling freshly poured battercakes and lemonade. "That's my twin brother, Ian. If Locklynn's wizard can manage to get on his good side, I might be willing to change my opinion of him."

His smile broadened. "It's already been done."

Ilene gave him a sidelong glance. "How do you know?"

"I let Ian win that scarf off me just this morning," Kipp said. "Plus, Gert's my cousin."

TOURNAMENT OF CHANCE: DRAGON REBEL

If Heather wins the Tournament of Chance, she'll be the first commoner to earn a place at court. Instead of a glorious victory, however, she's arrested and marked for execution. After a daring escape, she joins the Dragon Rebels, who seek to overthrow the despotic monarchy and restore the former kingdom of Ormaria. Amongst the rebels are three shape-shifting wizards who claim to be rulers from the past. On a perilous quest to free the wizards' magic, Heather must rely on her warrior skills, wits, and endurance to survive.

Keep reading for an excerpt...

TOURNAMENT OF CHANCE:
DRAGON REBEL

EXCERPT

Kneeling for what she hoped would be the last time, Heather scraped together a handful of dirt. Its drift indicated the westerly wind had kicked up again. Heather stood and adjusted her aim accordingly. *I am the arrow, and I will find my mark.*

Her arrow pierced the canvas of her target in the same hole as before. Even over the whoops and whistles of her supporters, Heather heard Joe yelling, "Yes!" behind her. She tried to give him a smile, but he was busy turning a handspring.

Then Felicia loosed her arrow. It hit the bull's eye, but off-center. The royals gasped in horror, and the commoners screamed in excitement. Heather's shock turned to bliss. She'd won the tournament at long last! Everyone fell silent when Felicia's head bent forward. She cupped her delicate fingertips over one of her lovely eyes. The royal surgeon examined Felicia and then had a word with the king. Heather was bewildered, as was Joe.

"What's going on?" he muttered.

Sir Fitzelle approached, a peculiar expression on his face. "I'm afraid you have been disqualified for cheating, Heather.

You threw dirt in your opponent's eyes. Her aim was off because of it."

Heather couldn't believe her ears. "I did no such thing!"

Joe was even more vocal. "That's complete dragon dung. Heather didn't cheat; I swear it! I was standing here the whole time."

Sir Fitzelle shot him a warning glance. "That's enough. It has been decided." He paused. "It's out of my hands."

Vibrating with shock, Heather stared at the ground. As Lady Felicia was declared this year's winner of the Tournament of Chance, the commoners began to boo. The sound began low but built until it resembled the groan of a hurricane. To show their dissatisfaction with the decision, people threw apple cores and rocks onto the field. Pushing and fighting broke out. When a few of the men stumbled through the rope barricades, the king's guardsmen closed ranks. Within short order, a phalanx of mounted guards joined the melee and created a buffer between the commoners and the royals. Even so, the booing grew louder.

In the meantime, the king, queen, and other members of court rose from their seats and filed toward the castle as quickly as their dignity would allow. The queen made no effort to mask her disgust. "Listen to those thugs! We try to be nice to the commoners, but they don't appreciate it."

"You don't understand, Chelsea. Commoners lack the capacity for higher thought. It's best to treat them like beasts in the field," the king replied.

If she'd been slapped, Heather could not have been more wounded. Tears pricked her eyelids. The king and queen were talking about her family, her friends—and her. When the king pointed an accusatory finger in her direction, however, she preferred the insults to what came next.

"Arrest her for inciting a riot," he told his guardsmen.

"What!" Heather gasped.

King's guards strode over to confiscate her bow and quiver.

Ustin and Obie tried to push through the crowd to come to Heather's aid, but they were intercepted by guardsmen. Despite Joe's protests, the guards took her into custody. As she was hauled away, Heather shook her head in disbelief. If this were a nightmare or some kind of joke, she'd long since ceased to be amused.

ABOUT THE AUTHOR

Originally from Southern California, Suzanne G. Rogers currently resides in beautiful Savannah, Georgia on an island populated by exotic birds, deer, turtles, otters, and gators.

ALSO BY SUZANNE G. ROGERS

FANTASY

Something Wicked in L.A.

Clash of Wills

Dani & the Immortals

*The Dragon Rider's Daughter**

Magical Misperception

Tournament of Chance: Dragon Rebel

*Whimsical Tendencies**

Royal Promenade

Yden Series

The Last Great Wizard of Yden (Book One)

Dragon Clan of Yden (Book Two)

Secrets of Yden (Book Three)

Kira (Prequel to the Yden Trilogy)

*Available in audiobook format

~

ALSO BY SUZANNE G. ROGERS

HISTORICAL ROMANCE

*My Fair Guardian**

*The Ice Captain's Daughter**

Lady Fallows' Secrets

*Spinster**

*Jessamine's Folly**

An American in Paris of the West

Rumer Has It

A Gift for Fiona

One Little Kiss

Courtship on Eaton Square

The Prettier Sister

The Glass Heart

The Mannequin Series

The Mannequin (Book One)*

Grace Unmasked (Book Two)

The Star-Crossed Seamstress (Book Three)

A Chance of Rayne (Book Four)

The Substitute (Book Five)

The Beaucroft Girls Series

Ruse & Romance (Book One)*

Rake & Romance (Book Two)*

Graceling Hall Series

Larken (Book One)*

Lord Apollo & the Colleen (Book Two)

The Vanishing Beauty (Book Three)

<u>The Gilded Age Series</u>

Duke of a Gilded Age (Book One)

Lady of a Gilded Age (Book Two)

*Available in audiobook format

www.ingramcontent.com/pod-product-compliance
Lightning Source LLC
Chambersburg PA
CBHW051522150726
47997CB00001B/350